D0482414

Mattie's Whisper

MATTIE'S WHISPER

Alice DeLaCroix

Illustrated by John Dyess

CAROLINE HOUSE

To Martha and Wyatt

Text copyright © 1992 by Alice DeLaCroix
Illustrations copyright © 1992 by John Dyess
All rights reserved
Published by Caroline House
Boyds Mills Press, Inc.
A Highlights Company
910 Church Street
Honesdale, PA 18431
DeLaCroix, Alice.
   Mattie's whisper / by Alice DeLaCroix; illustrated by John Dyess.
First edition.
[128]p. : ill. ; cm.
Summary: A young girl overcomes her own physical limitations through
care of an injured horse.
ISBN 1-56397-036-8
1. Horses—Fiction—Juvenile literature.   [1. Horses—Fiction.]
I. Dyess, John, ill. II. Title.
          [F]   1992
Library of Congress Catalog Card Number: 91-73885
First edition, 1992
Book designed by Charlotte Staub
Distributed by St. Martin's Press
Printed in the United States of America

Chapter 1

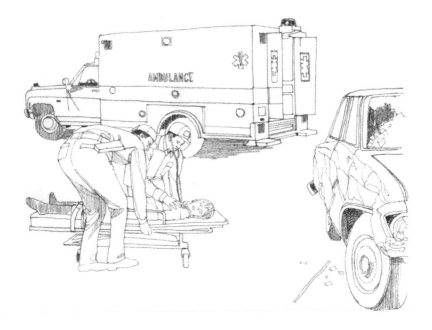

Mattie scratched Ted's star marking just below his forelock. The horse's eyelids drooped, and he blew a contented sigh.

"Don't make him too happy," joked Sherri, who was waiting in the saddle. "I've got to jump him in a minute, and I won't get a ribbon if Ted's half asleep!"

With a laugh, Mattie patted the horse on the shoulder, his steamy, salty smell reaching her nostrils. "You'll do great," she said. Sherri went to Winslow Jr. High with Mattie, but she was a year ahead, in eighth grade. Mattie liked knowing someone who took lessons at Gareth's stables; she didn't mind that her best friend, Jill, was not that someone.

For one thing, Jill was afraid of horses. For another, Mattie enjoyed having riding set her apart. In every other way, the girls were practically twins.

Dad handed Mattie her parka. "Let's leave," he said. "Things are getting icy out there."

Mattie had been dimly aware of the drumming sleet on the barn roof. The indoor arena could get so noisy in some weather, the horses spooked. They weren't bothered yet, so Mattie hadn't paid much attention. "Good luck," she told Sherri as she followed her father, dark sawdust licking at her black boots.

Mattie was eager to get home and share her success with Mom and her brother, Wayne. But she could see why Dad drove so carefully. In some places the road glistened with ice.

She laid her blue ribbons with their pretty rosettes and long streamers side by side on her lap. "Three firsts in Advanced! Not bad, huh?" She couldn't help crowing a bit.

"No," Dad answered.

Mattie sighed. After a horse show, she and Dad usually talked over some of the fine points. Though none of the family were riders but Mattie, Dad had seen enough competition to be a decent critic; his approval counted as much as any judge's.

The set of Dad's chin and the way he gripped the wheel showed he was concentrating on driving, the way she concentrated when she rode. It was the only way to be good, and Mattie Hall meant to be one of the best riders and trainers someday in the whole world. Well . . . in all of New York State, anyway. As soon as she filled that stall waiting at home with her own horse, she'd be one giant step closer to that goal.

She tugged her black velvet hard hat off. Mattie liked the tidy look of every strand tucked away while she rode, but it was a relief to let her blond hair fall to her shoulders again.

Suddenly Dad yelled, "Look at that guy coming!"

A large grey car zoomed toward them. Mattie gasped as it hit a patch of ice and shot sideways. She heard her father shout "No!" as he wrenched the steering wheel, trying to get out of the way.

Metal met metal with a bruising jolt. Their tiny car was shoved off the road and slammed against a telephone pole.

With the first jarring hit Mattie's mouth opened, but her scream was silent. She'd known nightmares like this, where she had to cry for help but couldn't get the sound out. Then pain streaked through her hip and up her back, filling her head.

Collision noise echoed through the frosted air, setting neighborhood dogs to barking, the last thing Mattie heard before blackness overcame her.

When she came to, Mattie was strapped down flat, and someone was lifting her into an ambulance. She couldn't stop moaning. Fear squeezed her. Was she going to die?

In a fuzzy, timeless world, Mattie heard the ambulance shriek to the hospital. White filled her mind when ceiling lights flashed by as she was rolled into Emergency and finally into a sterile-smelling room. Black floated all around her as she was filled with pain and fright.

Mattie had no idea how long it was until she latched

onto her mother's insistent voice.

"Mattie. Mattie, honey."

She felt Mom's kiss on her forehead.

"Mom?" She forced herself to stay connected.

"I'm here. I've been waiting for you."

"Waiting?" What was her mother saying?

"You've been in and out of consciousness and so dopey you haven't known much of anything." She leaned over to press her cheek against Mattie's.

Mom's softness reminded Mattie of bedtime, when her mother kissed her good night. She shuddered. Nothing else in the hospital room felt like home. Her chin quivered; crying was stupid, but she couldn't help it.

"You're going to be all right, sweetie," Mom crooned.

Mattie put her arms around her mother's neck and held on. "Sure am," she mumbled. But the tears kept coming. "I'm scared, Mom." Mattie didn't want to let go.

"I know, honey; you've had reason to be." She spoke gently near Mattie's ear, and Mattie felt less afraid.

Mattie released her so she could look into her mother's eyes—those deep brown eyes that had told her time and again that Mom loved her, or was furious with her, or had been hurt by her. After a minute, Mattie decided she could see nothing scary there. She believed Mom; she would get well.

But what was wrong with her?

She wiped a hand across her face. There was no problem moving from the waist up, but she couldn't move her legs. "I . . . what . . . what did I hurt?" She licked her dry lips. "Why can't I move? Are my legs broken?"

Crippled. Crippled. From somewhere deep inside, that word kept clanging at her. Mom might be fooling her after all. Her breath came in jerks. What did a kid like her know about reading eyes? Her mother was saying something, and she forced herself to listen.

". . . your legs are not broken. Your pelvis is." Mom talked slowly and deliberately, as she had done when she had taught Mattie how to iron a blouse or plant seeds in the garden.

Pelvis. Not legs. Mattie picked at the sheet under her hand, trying to keep her mind clear. Pelvis. She pictured the paper cutout skeleton she had put together for science class. The top of the leg bones matched the pelvis, Mattie remembered. It was big and important.

"You can't move because you're in traction," Mom said.

"Really?" Straining, Mattie pushed her chin as far onto her chest as she could to see the foot of her bed. "That's what all this contraption is?" She squinted toward the frame that rose above her, with ropes and pulleys attached.

"Kind of awesome, isn't it?" Mom gave Mattie a wobbly smile. Then she added, "It's going to hold you perfectly still while you heal. No wiggling allowed."

Mattie didn't want to hear any more. She let her head fall back. No pillow, even, she noticed. No comfort, period. She scanned the room. Tan drapes printed with rust and green circles hung neatly at the window edges, and large goose-feathery flecks of snow dropped past outside the single pane of glass. The walls were a mild green. But Mattie felt like an animal in a trap. If only she could curl up on her side in her usual sleeping ball and stop hurting.

She sighed. "I'm tired, Mom."

"Okay, honey. You rest." Her mother sounded weary.

For a short time visions of her hospital room flickered against Mattie's eyelids—the medicinal, closed-in smell of it strong in her nose. But soon she drove her thinking deeper, far down into her memory. At least remembering felt good.

She pictured herself, a little girl again, playing horse. Playing horse was as close as she could get to having one around during the long week between riding lessons.

It was even fun giving her brother, Wayne, horse rides. He was two years younger than she and sat lightly on her back. She held Mom's bathrobe tie in her mouth like a bit, and Wayne guided her with the two loose ends as reins.

It all worked well, Mattie thought; when her knees wore out, she had Wayne ready to fool around with the horse models she collected. From sofa cushions and wooden blocks, they built fancy stables and paddocks.

Lying stiffly in her hospital bed, Mattie fought to hold onto her safe memories. Some other muddled idea nudged in. There was something she must figure out. What was it? Right now she wanted only to think of a better time. Dad had said that one of the reasons they'd moved to the country was so they might have a horse. Dad had said.

Mattie's eyes flew open. "Mom!" she croaked. "Is Dad . . .? Where's Dad?"

Chapter 2

*F*ear stomped through Mattie. She could not — or would not — remember what had become of Dad after the crash. It seemed she had talked with him, but that may have been a dream too.

Mom sprang from her chair, dropping the crewel embroidery she had been stitching. She grabbed Mattie's hand. "Shh . . . calm down. Dad's home. He'll be here later today."

"He's all right?"

"Thank heavens." Her mother took a deep breath. "He

wasn't hurt badly at all." Mattie felt Mom tremble. This hadn't been any picnic for her, she guessed. "Don't you worry about him, sweetheart. We want you just to work on getting well."

Mattie kept hold of Mom's hand. Her skin was silky soft, but her grip was strong. People were always saying how sweet her mother was, but Mattie knew she was tough enough to lean on.

At five and a half feet, Mattie was already taller than her mother. Her legginess came from Dad. But what good were her legs now, long or short? She sure wasn't going to be jumping out of this bed anytime soon. Or riding. Or. anything!

Questions kept forming. Mattie couldn't relax. "How come Dad's so good, and I'm like this?"

Mom bit her lip.

"I mean, I'm glad, really glad, for him, but . . . Mom, we were in the same car. It doesn't make sense." Her feelings seemed tied to a seesaw; first she was scared rigid for Dad, and now she was angry with him. Mattie glared at her mother as if she were to blame for the mess she was in.

Mom's usually neat dark hair hung straggly, and her mouth made a hard narrow line. "You were just in the wrong seat, Mattie. On the telephone-pole side." She raised her shoulders and let them fall. "There are no reasons for things like this. They just are. I hate having you hurt so"—she stroked Mattie's cheek with the back of a finger—"but, we're lucky to have you," Mom said. Her eyes glistened, and she turned her head away.

The door to her room barely whispered. A man with heavy glasses slipped in. "Ah, Mrs. Hall. I was told you were here," he said, patting the pockets of his white coat.

Mattie sensed that she knew this doctor. Why? she wondered.

"I did want to have a few words with you and Mattie."

He must be one of the doctors who'd worked with her.

"Yes, Dr. Lasher?" Mom smiled too brightly at the neurologist who was handling her daughter's case.

"It will take some time for her fracture to heal, but she is young, and we expect no problem with the pelvis."

"I'm so thankful for that." Mom squeezed her eyes shut for a second and pressed fingertips to her mouth before she asked, "How long do you think, doctor?"

Did they have to talk about her as if she wasn't even there? It was her body, not theirs, Mattie thought. Why had this happened to her?

Mattie's temples throbbed, and she deliberately looked away from Dr. Lasher.

The doctor touched her arm and Mattie flinched, but he didn't seem to notice. "Six weeks in traction should bring the fracture reduction needed. Then another six to eight weeks on crutches should do it."

Six weeks! Dr. Lasher stood beaming down on her as though he'd said Christmas was coming tomorrow, when in fact he had told her she had to lie there for six weeks. She probably would be solid stone by that time.

He had said something about crutches though, hadn't he?

Mattie had to ask. "I will be able to walk—be like I was before this, won't I?" She could not use the word "crippled."

"At this point I see no reason why not, when you're totally recovered, Mattie. This kind of injury normally produces no paralysis."

Mattie was glad she had asked. Never to walk again was more scary than dying, she thought. Even the idea of walking funny forever and feeling people watching her was choking. The only time she wanted people watching her was when she was on a horse.

"I must explain though"—Dr. Lasher stepped away from her bed and spoke more to her mother—"there is the definite possibility of involvement of the first and second sacral nerves here, so we'll be watching for . . ."

More words, Mattie thought, but she didn't care to listen to any more. She drifted off again as Dr. Lasher's voice buzzed on.

Later that day Mattie struggled to come awake. Someone had called to her. It seemed she had to drag herself up from a deep, quiet well until she could surface and open her eyes. Focusing, she found Dad and Wayne watching her.

"Hi, pumpkin," her father greeted her with his baby name for her.

Mattie looked at his broad, rounded face, his solid shoulders and wide chest. When she had convinced herself he was all in one piece, she smiled and let the good feeling settle all the way to her toes.

He patted her hand.

Words weren't needed.

Then she noticed Wayne, uncommonly quiet, his shirt tucked in and all the buttons buttoned for once. He looked like a scared puppy! Mattie burst into giggles. She was surprised she could still laugh.

Laughing at Wayne was never a good idea. "What's so funny? What's the matter with you?" he asked.

"Hey, relax. You made me laugh, that's all. Laughter's

the best medicine. Right?"

"I guess." He returned her grin.

Mattie studied her father again. "You really okay?"

"Me? I'm fine. A few bruises and stiff and sore spots, but they'll clear up soon." He looked sideways at Mattie, and she nodded.

"You don't know how much I wish I were the one in that bed," he blurted, "with you standing here!"

Dad had said right out loud what she had been thinking. For a long minute Mattie held herself very still, ashamed to meet his eyes.

Dad cleared his throat. "Mattie?"

She looked at him then and found she could smile. It had been a stupid thought. She was all mixed up.

"You'll be all right, too, pumpkin. We'll help you all we can," he said. "It's just going to take some time."

She tried to find a chuckle again. "Some time! Twelve weeks—half of that time, Dad, just stretched out here like a bug in a collection. What will I do?"

"You're going to be real busy, I understand. In a couple more days, you'll be starting exercises. And schoolwork."

Mattie was surprised. "I was worried about school. Maybe Jill could bring my stuff and help me get it done?"

Dad nodded.

"I'd die if I missed so much I had to take seventh grade over."

"Not a chance," her father assured her with a grin.

"So," she said, "my vacation's almost over already, huh?"

"Looks that way, Mattie."

Mattie sighed as deep weariness recaptured her. So much had changed so fast and was going on changing for her, it made her exhausted just to think of it. One small minute of time had turned her life topsy-turvy. She shook her head to keep from slipping away from her family. She needed them now, even Wayne. She motioned him near.

"Does it hurt awful, Mattie?" He had that scared look back.

"Yeah. Sometimes it does," she said. "It'll get better," she tried to reassure him. She didn't want tenderhearted Wayne feeling sad over her. He'd had a cow when his little dog, Flossy, had broken her front leg last summer.

"Yeah," he echoed, "it'll get better," and shook his head hard as if to make it definite.

A spasm of pain hit Mattie. Where was the nurse with the medicine? She didn't have the energy to last through a good visit. She breathed the words, "Bring Tannie Annie. I want her," and then waved Wayne away.

Chapter 3

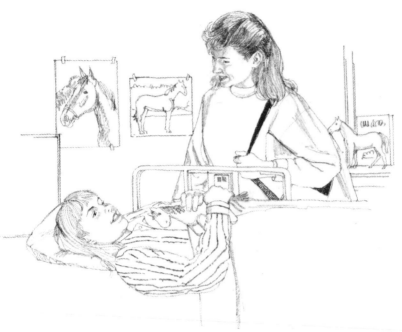

Mattie watched rain lace her window. She wished the sun would shine.

"Hi, honey." Mom had come to spend the afternoon with her. "Lousy day, isn't it?" she said, hanging her wet coat in the little closet.

"Yeah, lousy."

"I brought you something."

Her mother looked pretty today, wearing a red sweater that brightened her cheeks. From a canvas bag she pulled an old stuffed toy.

"Annie!" Mattie reached out; it was maddening not to be able to jump up. Her mother laid the tan cloth horse in Mattie's outstretched hand, and she cuddled it close. She had slept with that little horse ever since she got it in second grade as a birthday gift. "Oh, Tannie Annie," she murmured. Annie was barely three-dimensional, and the dark brown string mane and tail were thin from too much combing, too much loving. "Thanks, Mom."

"Wayne made sure I remembered to bring her. He went to your room and found her as soon as we got home last evening."

"He better not have gone through any of my things." It was her strict rule that her brother keep out of her room, a rule he gleefully broke anytime he could. He was the one who had named her room "the horse museum." Secretly, Mattie enjoyed the name; she did have horse stuff everywhere except for a slim path of blue carpet and most of her white-painted double bed. Right now she envied Wayne for being able to walk into her room when she was missing it so.

Mom dug again into her tote bag. "Wayne thought you might like a couple of your plastic models too."

"Great!"

Mom set a high-stepping white stallion and a grazing pinto model on the window ledge.

"Thank him for me, okay?" Now whether it snowed or rained Mattie had something good to see whenever she looked toward the window.

"That's not all," Mom said. She handed Mattie a pencil drawing of a horse.

"Ohhh, that's the best." She studied the picture. Mattie tried, but her horse pictures never looked real. Wayne's did. He could draw just about anything. "Hang it. Please?" She pointed to a spot on the wall that she could see easily.

When Mom relaxed into a soft chair, Mattie dozed, then chatted on and off.

"Look at the cards I got today, Mom." She waved her hand at the stack on her bed table. "There's a real funny one from Jill and Beth and Trina, and one from. well, you'll see."

Mom sorted through the greetings. "Oh, your riding teacher, Virginia, sent a card; isn't that nice!"

"Yes. That's the one I meant. Let me see it again." She reread the card, noting especially the handwritten part at the bottom that said "Hope to see you at the barn again soon." She had to get back to riding . . . just had to.

"I met a nurse I like this morning. Her name's Janice. She loves cats the way I love horses." A few seconds later she added, "And you know, the funniest thing, she purses her lips just so and there are little lines spoking out just like cat whiskers." She pursed her own lips, and her mother laughed with her.

"Janice got me to talking about horses . . ."

"Nothing hard about that," Mom teased.

She grinned. ". . . and thinking about what breed of horse I'm going to get — when I get my horse." Then a thought popped right out of Mattie's mouth without her knowing it had been there. "Is this costing an awful lot, Mom? The hospital and all? Can we still buy a horse?"

"Don't worry about it," Mom answered.

Don't worry about it? Mattie was ready for a horse. Everything was all set. And now this! She lay twisting Annie's poor tail. She would work hard at getting well just as fast as possible. Bring on the exercises, bring on the physical therapy. I can handle it, Mattie thought. Maybe it didn't have to take as long as Dr. Lasher said.

"I want a Thoroughbred," she said finally.

Her mom continued smiling. "Oh, look, you've got a visitor," she said brightly.

"Hi," came a soft voice from the doorway. There hovered Jill, a fat book bag slung over her shoulder.

"Well don't just stand there, come on down!" Mattie said, imitating the TV game show she and Jill sometimes watched, imagining themselves winning a little red motor scooter or a cruise to Jamaica.

Jill giggled and stepped closer. She was as tall and thin as Mattie. And they tried to keep their hair the same length, right at the shoulder.

"Why didn't you come sooner?" Mattie complained. "I've missed you tons! And school. And all the kids."

"Oof, heavy!" Jill swung the bag to the floor. "I know," she answered. "Hospitals sort of give me—you know—the."

"Creeps," the two said together and laughed.

"But, here I am. Hi, Mrs. Hall. I brought the books and some assignments."

"Jill, that's so helpful. I'm to see Mattie's teachers tomorrow. They'll give her as much work ahead as they can."

"It's only a couple of blocks out of my way, so I can come lots of days and help you, Mattie. We can go over the math problems and stuff, if you want to."

"Yeah, that'll be good. And we can talk."

"I've got the highest score in math class, so far." Jill went on, her eyes sparkling. "I want to win something at the awards night this year."

Mattie made a face. She used to compete with Jill in math, but this year she had lost interest. Seventh-grade English was more exciting than math now. And winning in horse shows was more exciting than anything in school. Still, she'd have to give Jill a bit of battle.

"How—how do you feel, Mattie?" Jill glanced at Mattie's rigging; she twisted a braided bracelet round and round her wrist.

"Did you make that?" Mattie took Jill's arm and held up the bracelet. She didn't like talking about how she felt. Not with a friend.

"I'll make you one like it. I just got the embroidery thread last week. I promised Arlene one, too."

A chill went through Mattie. Was she going to lose her best friend to Arlene Denton while she lay trapped here?

"But I'll do yours first."

Mattie smiled, but somehow she didn't feel very reassured.

"I'm going to run along now, honey," Mom said. She kissed Mattie's cheek. "Dad will see you tonight."

"Okay, 'bye." She looked toward Jill. "Let's start catching up on the math I've missed. Maybe I can work a whole problem before I conk out." She tried to joke, but she was feeling that terrible fatigue again.

Chapter 4

*D*ays and weeks merged together. Mattie struggled with the demands of being a patient. She filled empty hours with arm exercises and dreams of riding. Jill's visits made Mattie feel as if she'd been away from school forever. It sometimes seemed they had less to talk about than ever before. She had to get out of here soon, so she wouldn't be left behind.

At last, the full six weeks had passed. But now that it was time to be free, Mattie felt shaky. She reached for Janice's hand.

"Hey, take it easy, you guys," Mattie warned the two

attendants who were releasing her from traction. "I'm fragile."

"Aw, you're gonna love this," answered one of the men.

"You guys better know what you're doing." Bantering helped quell her fear.

"Do we know what we're doing?" one asked the other.

He laughed. "We'd better, because we just did it. You are free as a bird."

Mattie lay wiggling her toes. She imagined bending her knee, pulling her right leg out to the side. But she didn't really do it. Maybe she raised it ever so little. Maybe, she thought. "Well, well," she said and smiled. "When do I get up?" she asked Janice.

The nurse cranked the head of her bed up a tiny bit. "That'll do for starters, cookie. But just you hang onto your hat, because before you know it, you'll be doing it all."

Mattie closed her eyes to hold in the good feeling.

That afternoon Janice raised the bed further. "How's that?" She watched Mattie intently.

"It's nice. Wow, the room looks different from here." Wayne's horse drawings were even better from this angle. He had made a new one for Mattie each week.

"How's your head? Are you dizzy or light-headed?"

"No," Mattie said. "Am I supposed to be?"

Janice chuckled. "Well, sugar, it does happen. Your head's not used to being up there."

Soon her head was up, and so was she. Mattie sat in a chair, she stood in a walker, she learned more exercises.

Janice popped into the room one morning, pushing a wheelchair in front of her. "Okay, kiddo. It's time to do some real work." Janice expertly shifted Mattie into the chair. "All set, Mattie girl?" She seemed never to run out of pet names.

"I'm ready. Move 'em out." Physical therapy shouldn't be too bad. She thought it might hurt some, but she knew about pain already. She just wanted to get the rest of her twelve weeks behind her. Ohh, she couldn't wait to get back to school and friends and back home where she could be herself again.

Janice introduced her to Vince, a muscular young man who reminded Mattie of a gym teacher. "Vince will be your therapist, chick-pea. I'll be back for you in half an hour." She was gone in a blink.

"Hello, Mattie," Vince said.

"Hi," Mattie answered. All at once she felt like a little girl going into school the first day; all her boldness had fled somewhere.

Vince set a walker before her. "What's your favorite thing right now, Mattie? Clothes? Boys? . . ." He smiled.

"Horses." By the time that word was out, Vince had her scuffling along.

"Now aren't you glad we had you do all those exercises in bed? Your arms and shoulders have to be strong to take over for your legs for a while."

Mattie grunted. Yeah, those old dumbbells had done their job, she guessed. But when would her legs catch up?

When she reached a padded table, Vince said, "Let's see what we can do with this right leg now, Mattie." He drew an orange curtain around them.

With the session over, Janice wheeled Mattie back to her room. Mattie's insides felt tied in knots. I tried, I tried, I tried, she kept thinking. Why wouldn't it move? Vince had said she should try to flex her foot. She'd put her mind to it so hard she'd sweated with effort. But she couldn't make it move! Why had he asked her?

"Can't do it. It's too hard," she whined as she was settled into bed.

Janice glared at Mattie and pursed her lips. "Sweetie, you can do it. I know it, and before long you'll know it too."

Mattie threw Janice a "who asked you?" look.

"Didn't you have the guts to climb up onto an animal twice your height when you were a little kid? And haven't you had the grit to stick with that madness until you can fly over tall fences with a horse barely under you?"

It surprised Mattie right out of her self-pity to see Janice being so dramatic about her horseback riding.

"Am I right, or am I right?" she demanded.

"Uh-huh," Mattie answered sheepishly.

"Well, that's what this will take, Mattie. Guts and grit!" She softened her voice and finished, "I can tell you've got plenty of both."

It was embarrassing to go back to therapy after having left the day before not even speaking to Vince. But Janice's "guts and grit" kept coming back to Mattie. That could be her motto, she thought.

Guts and grit — you've got 'em, use 'em, she told herself as she said, "Hi, Vince."

From that day on, she refused to give up. Janice had been right. Mattie even mastered crutches in just three days. And that meant home! She was finally going home!

On the move again, her mind flew ahead. All the time she dreamed of riding. This was the longest she had gone without being on a horse since she started lessons years ago.

She wasn't through healing yet, though. It was the weirdest thing, to think "move" to her left leg, and it moved; then to think "move" to her right leg, and it barely twitched. Vince kept telling her, "Keep trying; it will come back in time." Guts and grit, Mattie reminded herself. Before the accident, she could tighten her thighs and calves so they were hard as rocks. She would get it all back, or burst trying.

Dr. Lasher came to her last physical therapy session. He watched her closely, then studied some papers Vince had handed him. With a frown he told Mattie, "I'll see you back in your room in a few minutes," then left. His dark look gave Mattie a tingle of fear. She shook it away.

When Mattie returned to her room, Mom and Dad were there. And by the time she was back into bed Dr. Lasher had shown up.

He greeted her parents and said, "Well, I trust you're ready to have Mattie back home with you."

"Absolutely," Dad replied with his short, nervous laugh.

"More than ready," said Mom.

The doctor let a little chuckle escape, then went on as serious as ever. "I realize that you've already been told she can leave tomorrow. I wanted to see you to explain her continued therapy."

"Yes, doctor?" Dad asked.

"You'll be bringing her in three times a week at first for therapy treatments here. See that she keeps up her exercises at home also. After a time, I'm sure, you'll only need to see us once a week, Mattie." He had turned to her. "How's that sound?"

Mattie had been eyeing her parents as they listened to

the doctor. Dad looked as if he were making mental notes of the instructions. Her mother fidgeted with an earring.

At first Mattie said nothing. Then she made herself ask, "Everything is back together?"

"Well, yes and no," Dr. Lasher hedged. "You see, we can tell definitely now that there has been stretching of the second sacral nerve group as I warned earlier there might well be."

Had he warned her? She sure didn't remember that. Her face must have told him so; he glanced quickly at the Halls for agreement.

Mattie saw her mother bow her head for a second, then tilt her chin high as she said simply, "Yes."

Dad's face looked stern. He nodded.

"You've noticed, I'm sure, Mattie, that your right leg is weaker than the left. And that your ankle won't flex easily?"

Now she kept her eyes on him. She thought, here it comes — the bad news!

The doctor eased his hand under her lower back. "Because the nerves right here have been affected, the muscles they control will show weakness, particularly your calf, hamstring, and buttock muscles."

Mattie felt the sweat pop out on her upper lip as she pictured herself dragging one flopping, half-useless leg. Sure, she knew her right leg wasn't improving yet, but she hadn't expected this! She was glad when Mom moved to touch her arm.

"What's it mean?" Mattie croaked.

Dr. Lasher frowned. "Only time will tell, Mattie. It takes time for nerves to heal. At worst, you will require a cane because of muscle wasting."

No way was she going to use a cane! Had this guy been in a school lately? She shook her head till tears came squeaking through her tight-shut lids.

Her mother tightened her hold on her arm. "Mattie?" she said.

Dad chimed in, "Mattie, you all right?"

But she couldn't answer. She whimpered, her hand pressed over her mouth, until, finally, she could speak.

The room was quiet when she asked, "What about at best?"

"At best, you will have some weakness and not be able to stand on tiptoes. It may limit your athletic endeavors but won't significantly hinder your walking, stair climbing, and so on." He clasped his hands together in front of him. "Just remember it will take time, Mattie, time before we know how much recovery your body can make."

Time! Wait and see. She was supposed to be well in another six weeks. That's what she had counted on. Now this! Keep on trying. Guts and grit, what a stupid, stupid motto!

Later, when she was alone, bewildered thoughts still whirled through Mattie's head. Her bones had mended—why couldn't her nerves? The pit of her stomach felt raw, she stewed so much.

Well, if waiting was what she had to do, that's what she would do. Maybe she was better than most kids at waiting; maybe that was her "gift." They had built the small barn and finished the stall more than a year ago, and she was still waiting to get a horse, wasn't she? "I have just begun to fight," she whispered to Annie. Hadn't some general or sea captain in history said that?

There were a lot of "athletic endeavors"—Dr. Lasher's

voice rang in her head—she didn't even like doing. Running, for example. As long as she could walk and ride horses she would be satisfied. And tomorrow she was going home.

Drowsiness slipped up on her as she listened to the late evening hospital sounds. The swish-swish of a nurse's walk down the hall melted into hushed words uttered somewhere along the way, and Mattie began her last night's rest in her hospital room.

Chapter 5

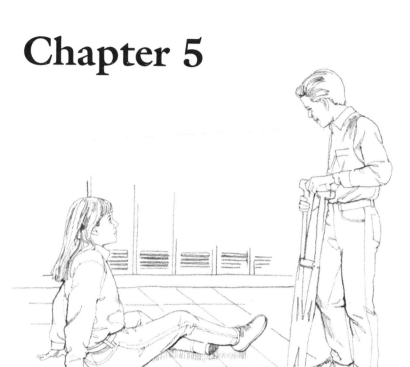

"**S**o, today I graduate, huh Janice? No more wheelchair taxis for me!"

Janice had pushed Mattie through the familiar halls of Mercy Central right up to the tall glass entryway. Outside, Mom had their car waiting on the curved drive. "Janice," Mattie said, staring at Janice's uniform zipper, "thanks for pushing me. And I don't mean pushing me in this chair."

Janice laughed. "Sure, doll. I told you, you had what it takes. I'll catch up with you for a hello when you're in for therapy. Count on it."

"You bet." Now Mattie could look her in the eye.

Mom helped Mattie transfer from the wheelchair to the car seat—not an easy maneuver, but they managed fine.

As her mother smoothly fitted her car into the stream of traffic on the expressway, Mattie's heart started a double-time march. She thought it might thump right out of her chest every time another car got close to them. Nothing had prepared her for this rushing down a highway; she had been thinking of being home, not of getting there!

At last, Mom exited the busy road onto a quiet back street. "Let's roll down the windows a little. It's pretty springy outside," she said.

"Yes." Mattie hoped Mom hadn't heard the shake in that one little word. She had to tell herself to let go before she released her grip on the car door handle.

Mattie rolled the window down and could almost see her fear fly away, the feeling was that strong. The fresh moving air smelled sweet.

When they turned up their long drive and made the curve that brought their house into view, Mattie shouted, "Home! I'm home! There's my window!" Waving her hands and craning her neck, she tried to see everywhere at once. "There's Wayne's bike—the trees. Hey, we have daffodils." Until this minute Mattie hadn't known how deep her missing had been.

She shrieked with delight when she reached the front door and saw the sign; it said MARVELOUS MATTIE in huge letters and was decorated with drawings of flowers and lots of horses. Her brother had painted on a roll of brown wrapping paper and stretched it across the house just above the door. How did he know that right then she felt like a marvelous Mattie?

Wayne and Dad helped Mattie up the step into the house. Dad just patted her hair. His hugs were usually bear tight. It's hard to hug someone on crutches, Mattie figured. Plus, maybe he was afraid of breaking her.

She was okay. She proved it by bumping along on her crutches, first into the family room, which radiated a cozy warm feeling, then into the living room, the prettiest room in the house. It seemed alive with Mom's green plants everywhere.

"Let's sit down and have some ice cream and celebration chocolate sauce." Mom headed for the kitchen while Dad escorted Mattie into the dining room and pulled a chair out for her. She touched the wood, a smooth and shiny cherry. Even a dining room chair could fascinate her today.

"Now watch this," she commanded, and she lowered herself into the chair. "Grace isn't part of my act yet," she joked.

"No sweat," countered Wayne, plopping into his own chair. "That's how I always sit down."

The whole family laughed and shared stories until suddenly Mom scowled. She pushed herself away from the table. Mattie must have looked as drained as she felt, because Mom said, "What have we been thinking? You need rest, Mattie."

Wayne held his bowl up as Mom crossed behind him to reach Mattie. "Can I have seconds, Mom?"

"Get it yourself," she answered shortly. "I'm helping Mattie to her bed."

"Okay." For a second Wayne seemed taken aback, then he started for the kitchen.

It had been such a long trip, reaching her room, her

horse museum, Mattie thought. She lavished long looks on all the things she had been away from. Her sheets smelled like mellow sunshine, like when Mom dried them on the line. Hospital sheets never smelled like that.

On the wall across from her bed was a huge poster of a life-sized head of a chestnut horse. It looked to one side out of its stall door with a patient, yearning expression, as if it were waiting for its master to come, and trusted she would. I'm back, horse; I'm really back, she thought.

"How's it feel?" Mom asked once she'd settled Mattie under her blankets.

Mattie smiled. Had anything ever felt better?

Mom kissed her. "You get some rest now." She turned to leave.

"Hey, Mom." Mattie stopped her. "You'd better let me change the calendar." The January horse picture and dates still hung on her wall.

"Sorry, honey," Mom said as she handed her the calendar. "This room just needs you."

"And now I'm here," she answered. She turned the calendar pages slowly, to see each picture she had missed. Then she studied the bold black numbers of today's date, March 25. After that came the 26th, the 27th, and so on. But she wouldn't think of tomorrow or what other days might bring. Right now was good. She would hold onto it.

Mattie did have to let March 25th go. Time passed quickly out of the hospital. At first she had needed tons of rest, but now she slept regular hours and felt almost normal—from the waist up, anyway.

Starting back to school had helped.

Jill hugged her and squealed, "I'm sooo glad you're back, Mattie! It's so great to see you!"

"You've seen me tons of times," Mattie corrected. Jill sometimes liked to make a big show.

"That was at the hospital and at your house. This is here." She hugged Mattie again.

Arlene Denton hung back, looking pouty.

"Can I try your crutches?" one of the guys asked. When she shook her head, he went on, "What'd you get hit by?"

"I heard you were run over by a horse! That so, Mattie?" someone else said.

"Me? Run over by a horse? No way!" She giggled with everyone else.

Mostly it was so good to be back that Mattie would have done a little dance—only, of course, she couldn't put her weight solidly on both feet yet.

After a few days, the attention dwindled; Mattie was just as glad. Sometimes she wanted to be invisible. Crutches made that impossible. Mattie couldn't wait to be free of them.

Jill walked with her to all of her classes but one, third period social studies. It was too far from her second period room for Mattie to make on time. Pierson, the teacher, didn't care, but it was mortifying having twenty-four pairs of eyes watch her clomp to her seat late every day.

Though she hated them, Mattie was really getting in tune with her crutches, and she swung through the wide hallway, gaining speed even in the crowd of students. Going to beat that bell today, she thought. She whizzed past two eighth-grade girls standing at their locker, but not fast enough to miss hearing them sputter with laughter. One called after her, "Wowee! It must be Tarzana, swinging through the jungle."

Mattie felt a blush explode all the way to her hairline.

She tried to slow down, lost her rhythm, and fell. The metal crutches clattered to the floor beside her. Someone tripped over them but kept on going.

Mattie lay on the cold tile, feeling her face burn.

"Here," someone said.

Mattie pried herself up enough to see a boy reaching down to her. He held her crutches. Still seething, she glared at the girls far down the hall.

The boy said, "Forget them. They're creeps."

With his help, she stood. He didn't seem bothered by her clumsiness. She felt bothered enough for both of them. "Pretty soon, I'll be off these."

"Yeah?" He sounded interested. "You all right now? I gotta get to class."

"Sure." She hadn't noticed how empty the hall had become.

"See ya." He sprinted off just as the class bell clanged.

He was tall, Mattie saw. Tall, and... and nice. Maybe she would see him. Maybe tomorrow on the way to class. And she wouldn't let herself look like an idiot again.

Next day when the second period ended, Mattie started her long trek. Taking a measured pace, she scanned the oncoming mob. There he was! He smiled, and she was amazed to see him break from the group.

"Hi, again," she said. "Thanks for yesterday."

He shrugged. "You're Mattie Hall, right?"

"Yes." She flashed a quick look toward his face. How had he known? He wasn't in any of her classes, but now she wished he were.

"I'm Ben." At that he took off again. "Catch ya tomorrow," he flung back to her.

She hadn't minded one bit getting to class late.

Yes, school's okay, she thought, lying in front of the TV that afternoon. But school's not everything. Horses are. She rolled onto her back and scrunched around for a position that relieved her aching. Horses and riding. It was an eternity since she'd touched a horse, felt a velvet-soft muzzle, scratched a broad blaze, rubbed fuzzy, pointy ears. The longing to be on a horse and feel that power beneath her, to ask for a trot or a canter with her thighs pressed just so against his belly—the longing was so intense she could taste it.

There was a girl at the stable who had broken her leg a couple of years ago. She had been in advanced classes but had to go back into beginners' for a while after her leg had healed. I wouldn't mind, Mattie thought. Anything just to get started again. When I go in for therapy tomorrow, I'm going to ask Vince about it.

But she didn't ask that next day. It was enough just to have Vince say, "Hand me those," indicating her crutches. "Now, walk to me."

And she had made it, limping tentatively. Vince caught her. "Good girl! You know what?" He held her at arm's length. "You tell me what."

"I don't need them anymore?"

"Right!"

"Right!" she shouted, and Vince actually hugged her.

Chapter 6

"'**A**re you always going to walk crazy like that, Mattie?' That's what Jill said, Mom, right out loud in front of everyone," Mattie wailed. She was too mad for tears.

Mom looked grim. "Well, what did the others say?"

"Oh, Trina called her a big mouth. But that doesn't matter. I hate her!"

"Now, honey . . ."

"And I am not going to school again. Ever!" Now she knew she didn't dare put her head down or tears would spill out. She'd felt so brave limping along without crutches. Sure her steps were wobbly and her hip jutted out, but she'd felt so proud — until Jill . . . .

Mom eased Mattie down onto her lap and rocked, making Mattie feel like a two-year-old. "Dear, dear Mattie," she cooed. "Such a lot you've had to take. You've come a long way, mostly on patience and willpower." She tightened her arms, and Mattie savored the quiet, safe feeling. "But—you know—you could use your crutches for these last couple weeks of school."

Mattie gave her a long look.

"No." She pushed herself out of her mother's lap. "I'm not going to get better if I baby myself." That's what Vince had said—not in those words—and she believed it. She would go back to school. No one was going to scare her out of getting well as fast as possible.

Jill's phone call came Saturday morning. Mattie had sort of expected it.

"You're still mad, aren't you?" she started.

Mattie humphed into the receiver. What was the clue? she wondered sarcastically. The fact that she hadn't said two words to Jill in two days, maybe?

"I'm sorry, Mattie. My mouth . . . I was just so surprised when I saw . . . ."

"Yeah, well I was surprised, too!" Surprised to walk and yet not really walk. Surprised at the betrayal in Jill's face.

"I really, really am sorry!" Then in a little voice, "I want us to be friends, Mattie. We've always been friends. And now I guess you won't be so crazy about horses; that's the only thing you and I didn't agree on."

"What!" Mattie exploded. "Not crazy about horses?"

"But, Mattie, I just thought . . . well, you wouldn't

be—the way you are if it weren't for horses, you know."

"Don't you know me at all? Maybe because of weather, or Mother Nature, or idiots who drive big grey cars, but never because of horses!"

"You've changed," Jill said.

"No. I'm still me. You're the one who's changed!" Mattie slammed the receiver down.

Friday when Mattie went to the hospital, Janice was waiting at the door of the therapy room. "Hi. You're looking good, doll. I checked the schedule when I came on my shift; saw you were due in about now. I've only got a second, but I wanted to see how you were."

"I'm fine." Mattie shrugged. "How are you?"

"Busier than a cat with kittens." She laughed. "You keep up the good work, sweetie, okay?"

Mattie nodded, her lips tight.

Her gaze held Mattie's. "I know you will," Janice said. " 'Bye for now."

This was the day she would ask Vince about riding. She waited till the end of the session. Her mind was frazzled from trying so hard to make things happen. It seemed her mind knew things her muscles didn't.

"My right leg is flunking out, isn't it? It just won't shape up." She slapped her thigh. "What's the matter with the stupid thing?"

Vince gave her one of his straight looks. "You know what's the matter." He settled beside her on the floor mat.

"The stretched nerves?" she said as half question, half statement.

"Yes. You're doing well, Mattie. You work hard."

"I know. I try." Her chin dropped. "But it's so slow." Then she raised her head. "Look, I've got to know when

I can ride a horse again. I can't squeeze with just one leg. I can't jump, can't even push my heels down, toes up . . . . " She searched his face for the right answer.

"You'll have to talk to your doctor—you and your parents." He sighed. "But, honestly, Mattie, I cannot imagine horseback riding as therapy for a patient in your condition. The pelvic fracture, those injured nerves." Maybe he didn't realize he was shaking his head all the time he spoke. "In a year, two years, those nerves might recover and your muscles will grow stronger. But until that happens you probably can't consider serious riding."

No, no, no! She didn't want to hear this! The thought of not riding had sneaked through her optimism once or twice, but she'd smacked it right down. Now Vince had said one year—two years. She ran her hand through her hair, damp with sweat, but she felt cold from her toes up.

The final word from Dr. Lasher was no riding for at least a year.

She slept fitfully that night, until morning air brushed her white curtains against the window seat.

This was usually the best few minutes of a day, when she hovered between sleep and wakefulness. But this morning she couldn't hold back the thinking.

Sunlight streaked the bottom of her bed, but the bright morning no longer felt good to her. Horses were her life! If they were now her past, what could her future be? She gazed around her room while she pulled on her old jeans. There were reminders everywhere in this horse museum. Listlessly she made her way down the hall.

At breakfast Mattie dutifully finished her egg and toast, then wiped a spot of runny yolk from her plate with her finger and licked it. As she left the table, she knuckle-thumped Wayne on the head.

He bellowed, "Cut it out!"

Mattie had counted on him to lose his temper.

"Wayne!" Mom scolded. "Don't be so loud."

"Yeah, well, she should keep her hands to herself," he fumed.

"No need to make such a fuss."

"No? Boy, you always take her side."

Mattie used the cover of the argument she had created to sneak a plastic garbage bag from the pantry. She slipped it into the waist of her pants and pulled her sweatshirt down over it.

Feat accomplished, she turned back. "I'm sorry, Wayne. I promise not to do that anymore."

He flashed an unbelieving look at her. She returned a bland, nonthreatening look to show she wouldn't fight, so he picked up his last piece of bacon. Half he stuffed in his mouth; half he poked under the table to Flossy.

"Mattie," Mom began as Mattie loaded the dishwasher, "Dad and I were wondering if you'd like to visit the stable. You must be missing the horses. Even if you're not riding, you might like to be around them."

Mattie blinked. Why now? Why today did she have to ask that? She could barely answer. "No. I don't want to." Without looking at her mother, she headed for her room.

Mattie closed her door firmly, wishing it had a lock, then stalked from wall to shelf to window seat. She stuffed all of her ribbons, trophies, calendars, posters, models, and books into the thirty-gallon bag, then poked and shoved until she had pushed the whole collection into the darkest corner of her closet. As an afterthought, she added her helmet, breeches, and boots. Then she saw her crop lying on the closet shelf. She crammed it into the bag, too. Finally she arranged a couple of big boxes full of old school things in front of it, then she curled up in a tight ball on her bed.

Mom knocked once, then stepped in. "I heard you moving around . . . Mattie, what have you done? All of your horse things . . . ?" Disbelief flooded her face.

"I don't want to see them," Mattie answered. "I'm not a horse girl anymore." She hurt more with every word, but somehow couldn't stop. "And I'm not Marvelous Mattie, either," she added. "Just Mattie the Mess!" She saw the look of concern fill her mother's eyes. Mattie couldn't help it. She rolled over to face the wall. "I—I've got to figure out what I am, Mom. Okay?" She sounded dull and weak.

Her mother hesitated, then answered in a tiny voice. "Sure, honey . . . sure." She closed the door quietly when she left.

All through that weekend Mattie moped. Admitting defeat had been so hard. More than once she stood poised at her closet door, tempted to retrieve all that she was trying to put behind her. But she held fast. Horses were not her thing anymore.

She stood before her door mirror, trying to see who was inside those hazel eyes staring back at her. Jill was right, she thought. I have changed. She clutched Tannie Annie. She hadn't gone into the bag; that would be impossible. Mattie told herself Annie wasn't really a horse. She gave up; she was nobody now. But one thing for sure, Jill was not going to know Mattie was not a horse girl anymore. How could they ever have been best friends? she wondered. Anyhow, it didn't matter. Nothing mattered.

Chapter 7

*A*t last school was out for the summer. Mattie guessed that to others she seemed happy enough, but it was an act. She had to keep pretending, not just to other people, but to herself, making sure no forbidden horsey stuff appeared.

Once a week Mattie still went for therapy with Vince. And she faithfully did her exercises at home. She had to get control over her body again. Nothing would stop her trying.

Otherwise, she spent a lot of time alone in her room.

Wayne burst in on her there one morning. "Mom says she'll take me to get Brent, 'cause he can come over today. You want us to get Jill, too?"

Mattie laid her book on her chest and glared at Wayne.

"Go on. Call her. Why don't you?"

"Because."

"Why?" Wayne kept coming closer until he sat on Mattie's bed. He looked sad.

"Get out!" She meant to kick him off her bed, but her leg gave a wimpy tap. Quickly she grabbed her book; the words swam before her eyes. Wayne couldn't understand in a million years!

At least her brother left in a hurry.

After that, one meaningless day smudged into the next, till Mattie felt close to exploding with frustration. She began to think there must be another way. This just wasn't working.

Then one day in early July, Sherri phoned. She wondered how Mattie was getting along. "I've missed you at the stable. There's a show there this Sunday," she said, "but I can't go. My mom has decided we need a vacation. Groan!"

"A vacation's nice, don't you think?" Mattie asked.

"I guess—yeah, really, I just hate to skip a show and lose the points I might win." Then Sherri laughed. "Oh well, probably wouldn't get much anyhow."

"Sure you would," Mattie said quietly. She was picturing past shows. Sherri was a good rider, though Mattie had won more than she last year.

When the call ended, Mattie realized she was letting horse memories back in. She could not get the stable and show out of her thoughts all day.

That evening she sat silently at dinner, pushing her green beans around on her plate. Finally she took a deep breath and said, "Dad, I was talking to Sherri, the one who takes lessons at Gareth's stables, and she says there's a show there this Sunday. Could I go?"

Dad stopped chewing, his eyebrows arching in surprise. He swallowed before he replied. "Mom and I thought . . . you're sure you want to go?"

Mattie looked down at her green beans. "I'm sure." Actually, she was never sure what she wanted anymore. But she had gotten up the nerve to mention the show, and she wasn't going to waver. Besides, now that she had said it out loud, it seemed exactly the right thing to do.

"What do you want to go for?" Wayne asked. "You said you didn't want to hear the word 'horse' again."

Mattie scowled. Why couldn't Wayne keep out of her business?

Dad reached out to touch Mattie's hand before she flared up at her Wayne. "If you think you can go it alone, I'm all for it. Mom and I have to be in town that afternoon, but I could drop you off."

"Sherri will be there, won't she?" Mom put in.

Mattie shook her head. "She's going away on vacation. But I don't mind—really."

"Let me go too, Mattie," Wayne volunteered. He wolfed down his chocolate pudding, drawing a glare from Mom, and pretended indifference until Mattie answered.

"Sure. Why not." Wayne, mouth and all, was good to have around when she wasn't feeling too certain of herself. Right now, though, she was smiling from the inside out for the first time in ages.

At bedtime Mattie walked toward her mirror. She didn't

think she would attract too much attention at the horse show. Her ugly limp was at its worst only when she rushed or was overtired. She gave a couple of giddy twirls before the mirror, then climbed into bed, pleased with herself. How could she feel so good? she wondered. Did it mean finally she was doing the right thing?

Sunday morning came alive with the crow of a neighbor's rooster.

Mattie was eager when Dad left her and Wayne at Gareth's. Her stable! How could she have stayed away so long?

The trimmed grass accented with rich red geraniums mimicked Gareth Stables' colors. Several riders were mounted and waiting their turn to enter the outdoor ring. Mattie avoided the show ring. Watching other people ride was going to take some warming up to. She made her way slowly to the big white barn that housed the indoor ring and horse stalls. Wayne trailed behind.

She passed through the rolled-open doors, into the shelter of the barn. The hushed cathedral feel enveloped Mattie. She'd always loved smelling horse. Now she felt wrapped in the aromas and the quiet sounds. Mattie soaked up the peace of the barn. It seemed impossible that she had ever been away.

Most of the lesson horses were tacked and being ridden in the show, but there were a few privately owned and boarded horses in stalls. They greeted Mattie's pats on their soft muzzles with curiosity. A chestnut mare strained her neck over her stall door, sniffing for any treats that might be coming her way. Mattie patted her silky neck.

"Just look at her eyes, Wayne. You can see the intelligence."

"Yeah, yeah. But they just called class 12 next on the loudspeaker. The sheet says that's advanced jumping." He looked at her expectantly. "Let's get over to the ring and see some action." He moved to the doorway.

Mattie looked at her feet, absentmindedly stroking the mare. Ordinarily on show day, she would be wearing shiny black boots, not scruffy grey-white sneakers. Strange. She shrugged then and followed Wayne.

This was what she had come for, wasn't it? In this class she would watch kids she had competed with. She'd wanted her new-found peacefulness to stay with her, but her heart had started flipping, the way it always did when she was about to perform.

Wayne had barged ahead but turned to wait for Mattie, an anxious frown creasing his forehead. My mother hen, Mattie thought. She kept as smooth a step as possible, though she wanted to hurry.

They found a good viewing spot at the rail. Mattie chose to watch from the side of the ring so she could count the strides between jumps more easily. She studied the gates with a calculating eye: a brush box, an in-and-out, a latticework fence, a coop, and a square oxford. It was a familiar setup: challenging, but not too difficult.

Just then the first rider was announced. Mattie sucked in her breath when she saw the horse. It was Bill, the last horse she had ridden before the crash. Still, she was glad to see him again. Good old Bill—his registered name was something like Regal Overdrive. He had a miserable, lumpy canter but always took the gates beautifully.

Quickly Mattie shifted her attention to the boy on Bill. She checked the set of his heels in the stirrups, watched the position of his hands, the slant of his back. Her fingernails dug into her palm and she grunted when the rider cut his first corner short. That was so easy to do, she knew. You've got to guide that horse all the way, she thought.

Each gate would be jumped twice, and by the second time around, Mattie was so involved she felt for herself the boy's graceful bend as Bill left the ground. She was so intent that she didn't realize she was dripping tears until Wayne tapped her arm.

"Let's get outa here," he said.

"No!" Parents and friends were applauding the rider, and Mattie wiped her face on her shoulder, hoping no one noticed. "No. It's okay. I'm okay." She couldn't say more. She had come back to her horse world. It made her happy and it hurt. She knew now that riding wasn't everything, but she couldn't give up horses. At last she was being honest.

They stayed on for the rest of the show, and it was the best thing Mattie had done since coming home from the hospital. She was letting go of the awful, heavy thing that had been dragging her down. She was a horse girl; just one of a different kind now. She'd jumped her own fence and landed free.

"Nice job, Sarah!" Mattie heard herself shouting. She'd shared many a ride with Sarah, and Sarah had just been handed a well-earned red ribbon. She wasn't usually bold enough to make a racket, but today she wasn't herself. Or, maybe, she was especially herself.

Wayne began to get itchy when he could see that Mattie no longer needed him. Fortunately, Mom and Dad drove in to pick them up before he took to biting his nails. But at the same time Virginia, Mattie's riding teacher, strode up to them. "Mattie. It's great to see you here." Her smile lit her tanned face. "How are you doing?"

Mattie's heart did a little skip, and her words came out with too much air. "Fine. Really fine now."

"Great! Will I be seeing you at lessons before long?"

"No." She swallowed, then plunged ahead. "I'm not supposed to ride anymore. At least not for a long time."

"Oh. Oh, I see." Virginia's eyebrows went up, signaling that she didn't know what else to say.

"I have to go now," Mattie said. Her parents and brother were already waiting in the car. She didn't move. "Wish I didn't have to go. It's great being back here." Why was she blabbing so?

"Well, I am short a stable hand. Would you be able to . . ." She started over. "Would you want to stay and help get a horse or two untacked and groomed?"

Mattie took no time for thought. "Sure! I'd love to. Let me tell Dad." She rushed to the car with no thought of how awkward she looked.

Virginia called after her, "Hank can drive you home."

"Dad! I'm going to stay awhile and help out in the barn," she shouted. "Imagine, me with a horse in my hands again!"

Dad grinned. "Fine. See you in a couple of hours, pumpkin."

He didn't even remind her not to overdo. She must be finally well!

Chapter 8

Mattie groaned as she climbed into Hank's dusty pickup later that evening. She had hustled from stall to stall to tack room, lugging saddles, hanging bridles, currying weary animals, picking hooves. Now she leaned her head against the window as Hank crawled into the driver's side.

"You're one pooped gal, ain't ya?" He laughed. "But I've never seen a happier face on a working lady before, I declare!"

Mattie smiled through her tiredness. She had seen Hank

around Gareth's—the label All-Purpose Handyman seemed to fit him—but she had never talked with him. His attitude made her feel comfortable, though.

Closed up in the truck cab, he was magnified in size. His great hands covered the steering wheel.

"I loved being with the horses," she volunteered.

"Yes, I reckon you did. I caught sight of you giving 'em neck hugs and rubbing 'em. Scratched old Red behind the ears until I bet he thought he'd died and gone to heaven." He laughed again and winked at her.

Mattie blushed, surprised that he'd noticed her.

They rode silently for a time. Mattie's mind hummed contentedly despite her aching body.

When Hank spoke again his jovial mood was gone. "Sometimes I think we're awful fools to care so much for horses. Just breaks your heart sometimes." He shook his head and blew out a long stream of air.

Mattie thought she knew more than anyone about heartbreak over horses, but it seemed this man carried his share of sadness, too. Why? she wondered. She wasn't brave enough to ask but looked at Hank, hoping he would go on.

He heaved another deep sigh. "There's this fella I know; he's got himself a nice little string of horses he takes around to the race tracks. Boy, it burns me just to think about him!" He flexed his hands over the steering wheel. "Anyway," he said, glancing at Mattie, "I shouldn't be telling you this. You likely got your own problems."

"Trust me, someone else's problems would be a nice change." She couldn't let him stop now; this sounded interesting.

So Hank talked on, as though he'd been needing a

listener like Mattie. "He's got a four-year-old red roan mare, a real darling she is. And he's raced her a lot. Over-raced her, I think, but I'm the first to admit I'm no expert. Anyhow, she's developed something called navicular disease. It bungs up her front feet something pitiful."

"You mean she can't race anymore?"

"Race? Shoot, no!" Hank's face turned scarlet with the force of his reply. "She's crippled up. Can just about walk, is all."

Like me, Mattie thought.

Gesturing with hands and head, Hank continued. "The smart thing to do would be for this fella—Jacobs is his name—to use her as a brood mare, give her a happy, useful life. He's one of them fellas usually does everything for the dollar, but not this time. He's got it into his head to put her up for auction." He gave Mattie a dark look. "And I don't mean any fancy, highfalutin auction. She'll be going to some danged dog food company, for sure," he added and grimaced.

Mattie had been staring at Hank as if reading his words on air. Now she blinked hard with the effort of understanding. Why did a fine young horse have to die because she couldn't run races? Mattie's palm rubbed at the knee of her own weak leg. It wasn't the horse's fault. It was so unfair!

They had been poking along the highway, its edges white with Queen Anne's lace, and she realized where they were just in time to direct Hank, "Turn in at the next driveway."

By then it was late evening, and the sun had dropped to that level where it shone sideways through all the summer's green and tinted the world golden for a few moments. Mattie saw the splendor, the magic, of it but couldn't feel it as she usually did. Nothing could seem beautiful right then.

Hank pulled up to the house, idled the engine of his rattly truck and tried to apologize. "Now see what I've gone and done. I've taken the smile right off that pretty face. Knew I shouldn't be going on that way."

"Hey, it's okay," Mattie assured him while carefully stepping down from the cab. "Thanks for the ride."

Then, as Hank shoved the stickshift into reverse, Mattie suddenly shouted, "Wait! Could you take me to see her?"

Hank stuck his head out the window. "What?"

"Could I see the mare before auction time?"

Hank shook his head, a slip of grey hair falling across his forehead. "Oh, now, girl. You best put her out of your mind. There's nothing can change things."

Mattie faced Hank squarely. "You say you're sorry you brought it up. Well, the way to make it up to me is to take me to see her before she's sold." She had learned that you can change some things. You don't have to lie down and give up.

Hank was smiling now. "I'd like to do that. But I still don't see just why you'd want to see her."

Mattie shrugged. "You made her sound special, and she means something to you. I'd like to see her before she's gone, that's all." Mattie studied the small cracks in the blacktop driveway, overwhelmed finally by her own mouth.

Hank slapped the side of the truck and chuckled. "Well, I will, if you want to so much," he said.

Mattie stood straight. "Great!"

"Check with your pop, and if he says it's all right, I'll

drive you down there tomorrow."

Mattie waved and turned toward the house. All at once she felt she had used every last morsel of energy. Her entire body hurt, and her legs felt almost as wobbly as they had two months earlier. Tired as she was, though, when she thought of the horse and the auction, her mind raced with possibilities. Probably there wasn't anything she could do for the mare, but she did sound wonderful, and at least Mattie could see her.

The next day, as Hank pointed his truck up the narrow drive toward Jacobs's farm, Mattie felt tense. The thickly treed landscape gave way to wide fields with endless fencing and immaculate buildings fronted by lush grounds.

Hank parked beside the main stable. "Well, what do you think? This upper stratosphere make you light-headed?"

"You didn't tell me it was so grand." Though still sore from yesterday's work, Mattie sprang to the ground.

She started after Hank; he had moved off in long strides to find his friend Lars, who was stable manager there. The spell of the barn caught her. Mattie imagined who might occupy each roomy stall, using the gleaming brass name-plate beside the door as a guide. Even the hinges and latches looked like expensive brass. It would be great to have a place like this.

When she caught up to him, Hank was talking with a man smaller than himself who had a wiry, hard-muscled look. Hank introduced her and explained, "I brought this gal to see a horse."

"Well, now. What else would you see on a horse farm—kangaroos?" Lars broke into a wheezy laugh that sounded like a whinny and clapped Hank on the back.

He gave Mattie a kind look. "Never mind me, Miss. I'm always trying to get one up on old Hank here." The two men poked at each other like a couple of kids. "What horse did you want to see? Most of them are out on the racing circuit this time of year, you know."

She glanced at Hank for support and blurted, "The red roan mare that's to be killed." That's how Mattie thought of it, but why had she said it?

"Killed?" Lars repeated, surprised. "We don't kill horses here." The twinkle left his eyes.

Mattie wished that Hank would help her. He had clasped his hands behind his back, and he stood looking at her with a patient half-smile. She hadn't shocked him, and he was giving her her lead. "No, of course not. I'm sorry." She raised her chin. "I mean the one who is going to be auctioned because she has bad feet."

"You mean Whisper then," Lars said.

Again she looked at Hank, who nodded. "Yes. May I please see Whisper?"

Chapter 9

Whisper. What a lovely, lovely name. Hank hadn't told Mattie the mare's name.

"She's a beauty, you'll see, Mattie." To Lars, Hank added, "I got to jawing about this horse yesterday to Mattie, and wouldn't nothing do but she get a look at her."

Lars scuffed his work boot across the floor. "'She's in a back barn." As they walked, Lars talked uneasily. "I've got my orders to take this mare to auction Saturday. I don't expect Mr. Jacobs wants me showing her off."

Mattie watched the ground but listened intently.

"Why not?" Hank spoke her thought.

"She's in disgrace, you see. Banished. That's why she's out here alone," he explained as they entered a grove of pine trees and weedy brush.

"In disgrace! Well, I never...." Hank snorted.

"Me neither," Lars said, rolling back the door to the small barn. "But this Jacobs is a strange one. Whisper can't do what he thinks she ought to do, so he wants her out of his sight and off his property, the sooner the better."

The barn was little more than a shed, half hidden by the tall grass and weedy thickets. The men fell into Mattie's silence as they entered. If the main stable had spelled rich, this place spelled neglect. A slant of sunlight splashed through the opened door onto the center of the floor, but corners remained deep grey.

Mattie's eyes adjusted to the dimness. Then in a dark corner she saw the horse. It was tied—like a prisoner, Mattie thought—with no light and no decent ventilation.

Whisper stood, head lowered. Mattie eased up and reached a hand out. The horse swung her head up and turned soft, dark eyes toward her.

"Whisper? Hi, Whisper," Mattie crooned. She pulled a piece of carrot from her jeans pocket and held it out in her palm. The mare whinnied and lipped the treat into her mouth. Okay! Mattie thought. She's got spirit enough to appreciate a good carrot. Mattie patted Whisper's neck and stroked her head, all the while talking quietly to her. The mare showed no nervousness but leaned into Mattie's rubs.

Remembering Hank and Lars, Mattie asked, "Can't we take her outside? Walk her a little?"

"Sure we can. She needs to be out." Hank started for the horse, but Lars had folded his arms and stayed where he was. "What's the matter?" Hank demanded.

"My orders are to keep her in. And when Mr. Jacobs is on the farm, as he is today, he keeps a close eye on things," Lars said.

Mattie gaped at him, feeling as stubborn as he sounded. Hank said no more either, but he joined Mattie in staring at Lars.

"But I don't think much of his ways right now." Lars marched to the tie-up. "We sure will take her out. Truth is, I've been sneaking her out for a little fresh air anytime I know the boss is away."

"Now that's more like it." Hank had his grin back.

"Understand, this is the first time I've known the boss to be downright inhumane. But, by George, if a second time comes around, I quit. I need the job, but not that much."

Hank grunted approval.

Mattie stuck close by Whisper as she followed Lars outdoors. The mare limped, favoring her front feet. She was in such obvious pain, it made Mattie's heart feel all tight to see this horse hurting so much.

Whisper never should have been put out in a dark shed alone, left to suffer. Mattie thought the horse was more courageous than she. She would have bitten the first person who showed up if she had been treated this way.

In the sunlight, Whisper's coloring became clear for the first time. Not your usual bay or chestnut or even grey, she was a red roan as Hank had described her, with flaxen mane and tail. The real red of a blood bay plus white hairs mixed in combined perfectly with her light points. Whisper would have been exceptional for her color alone.

But she carried smudges of dried dirt on her legs and hindquarters and obviously hadn't been groomed recently. Mattie jammed her hands into her empty pockets. If only she had brought a brush with her, she could help Whisper feel better.

Whisper tossed her head and neighed at the breezes, then made her way to a stand of thick grass. She yanked hunks and tucked them tidily into her mouth.

Apart from her, Mattie couldn't stop an "Oh, wow!"

"Didn't I tell you she's a beauty?" Hank couldn't stand still.

Mattie nodded.

Whisper stepped clumsily forward, and Mattie remembered: Whisper was about to be sold. Worse—killed. "Why?" she blurted. "I don't understand. A body like that looks like it could fly down a race track. Didn't she win?"

"She was winning, all right," Lars answered. "That's why he raced her so much. She had speed, for a fact."

"Hank says she would make a good brood mare. Why won't Mr. Jacobs do that?" Mattie had been thinking about what could be done. She kept looking straight at Lars. "At least sell her to another breeder?"

"Well, now, the way I figure it, the one thing more important to the boss than money is his pride. I hear through the grapevine that he was big-mouthing last season how Whisper would be a serious contender for the Triple Crown. Imagine that?" He gave Hank a significant look. "So when she went lame it was like a personal insult to him. I guess he would really like to see her go for dog food." He let his shoulders slump. "Maybe you're right, in a way, about us killing horses."

Mattie's stomach lurched. It just couldn't happen. She gritted her teeth and kicked dirt a minute while her mind worked away.

"When is the auction?" she asked finally.

"Saturday, coming up," Lars said.

"I've never been to a horse auction. Can anyone go, or is it just for certain people, like the dog food buyers?"

"Oh, no. Anyone goes that wants. Won't be much crowd left except the meat men, though, by the time Whisper is taken in."

"Why?" Mattie couldn't believe how bold she was being with an adult she had just met, but she had to find out more.

Lars scratched his chin. "The registered horses are auctioned first, and that can take the better part of a day. Then the grade horses, and at the tail end, the unsound ones. That's when I'll take Whisper in the ring."

Mattie bit her lip. "But, she's registered, isn't she?"

"Yep. But, remember, she's also lame," Lars went on. "Folks don't generally buy a horse through an auction unless they're experienced enough to spot a good animal on short acquaintance. They'll see plain as day she is lame—we ain't allowed to dope her—and a lot will even figure navicular disease with a good look at her. Vets still don't know for sure if it's an inherited tendency. So it's not likely anyone would want her for a brood mare even, as you were saying."

"Anyhow, you said Jacobs wants her to sell for dog food," Hank added bitterly.

Lars simply nodded.

A feeling that had rooted somewhere inside her began

to bloom into a solid plan. Maybe it could work. Mattie said, "But it is possible for someone to try to beat out anyone else in buying Whisper."

"Sure. An auction's an auction." Lars seemed to catch up to her line of thought. "Shoot, there isn't any law says she has to go to a meat buyer."

"What are you thinking, girl?" Hank asked. He rubbed Whisper and turned a hopeful face toward Mattie.

Mattie's pulse was racing, but she had to appear cool now. Innocently she answered, "Just curious."

Lars shrugged. "I should put her inside now and get back to work, if you don't mind, Hank."

"I reckon you should. Thanks a heap for showing her to this young'un." He seemed pleased, his usual jolly self. "Now she has one mighty fancy horse to remember."

"Yes, thank you very much." Mattie remembered her manners. She took the lead rope, giving it a couple of firm tugs to get Whisper to leave her feast, then walked along beside her. Inside the stuffy grey envelope of a shed, Mattie blew softly into Whisper's nostrils. That's the way Indians used to make friends with horses, she had read. The mare responded with a quiet whicker and nuzzled against Mattie.

"Bring her some fresh water, won't you?" It was pretty nervy of her, telling Lars what to do, but she didn't care.

"Yes, I'll be doing that." Lars rolled the door closed behind them.

Mattie had to force herself to walk away from Whisper. She yearned to turn back and find Whisper following her. A huge need had been opened up inside Mattie. By the time she reached the pickup truck with Hank, something new had begun to fill her. Hope.

Chapter 10

*A*s they chugged toward home, Hank quizzed Mattie. "You're thinking of trying to save that mare, aren't you?"

She decided he had to be trusted. "I don't know if I can." She shoved her hair off her forehead. "But I sure am going to try!"

Hank cheered. "Atta girl! You've got spunk. Yep, a heap of spunk."

Mattie grinned. "Thank you, sir. I like you, too," she said. They laughed together.

It felt great knowing at least one person was behind her. She hardly dared think what Mom and Dad were going to say.

"Say you manage to buy Whisper, would you be able to keep her?" Hank asked more soberly.

"We've been planning to get me a horse for a long time." Well, he didn't have to know everything about that.

"You know anything about navicular disease, Mattie?" His clear blue eyes held her.

"A little. I've read about it."

Hank continued as though determined to help her through the bad part. "Then you know that she'll not be a mount for you. You'll not be riding her. Just taking care of her, is all."

"I can't ride anymore. At least not for a long time yet. And I've got plenty of caring to give," she answered in a way that showed for her the subject was closed.

When Hank let Mattie off at her house, he wished her luck and gave her a thumbs-up sign.

Gravel crunched under the truck tires as Hank backed into their turnaround. He shifted gears to move on down the drive.

The churning atmosphere in the house quickly told Mattie that this was not the time to talk to her father. His face wore its strained look that a day at his office sometimes left, and he was growling at Wayne about some unmowed lawn. Wayne was busy making limp but equally loud excuses, and Mom stuck in words meant to placate both but that just kept things riled up.

The argument stopped long enough for Mattie to say, "I'm home."

"Good. I'm glad you're back," Dad answered, still with an edge to his voice.

"How was it?" Mom asked.

"Fine." The word ended high, but she said no more.

Dad's voice halted Wayne, who was attempting his escape past Mattie. "If you get out there right now, you can have that lawn finished before dinner." He snapped open his evening paper.

"Why do I have to do everything? Now you make me do her half and mine, too." Wayne stabbed at Mattie with dagger looks as he passed her. "Mattie, Mattie, Mattie!" he shouted. "Everything's Mattie." He streaked out of the house.

Mattie slipped away to her room, guilt washing over the good feelings she'd come home with. That dumb Wayne. It wasn't her fault she couldn't walk behind a mower. Let him go out and get his legs wrecked! She gasped at her meanness, ashamed. "I didn't mean that, Annie," she told the little horse. "Not for a second." She lay stroking Annie and soon thought only of Whisper.

Wayne had been invited to Brent's for dinner and a sleepover, Dad had an early meeting that made him rush through his meal, and Mom was distracted with all the comings and goings. Mattie decided it would be best to wait until morning to divulge her plan.

She had a hard time getting to sleep that night and woke early the next day. She wasn't going to drift back to sleep today as she usually did. Instead she plotted, then rose to share breakfast with Dad.

Dad was a champion early-morning person. The world was new to him each sunrise, and he was unfailingly glad about it. Mattie knew he enjoyed company with his cereal and juice but seldom got any during school vacation weeks. It might help her case by getting up to eat with him.

She poured herself a bowl of cereal and tried to act natural, though her stomach was doing loopdy-loops.

"Dad, the horse I saw yesterday is really wonderful. Her name's Whisper."

"Whisper," he repeated. "It was nice of Hank to take you. You like him—Hank?"

She nodded.

"Me too, when I've talked to him at the stable. You know me, I'll talk to anyone half willing. And Dick Gareth said he was a good man."

Mattie smiled. Dad was definitely in his good morning mood.

"What was she like—this Whisper?" he asked between bites.

That was just what Mattie wanted to hear. She gave up pretending to eat, and all of Whisper's virtues and beauties tripped off Mattie's tongue. "And it's totally unfair and—and ridiculous for that horse to die! I know you'd agree if you saw her, Dad."

"Probably would. It doesn't sound like the owner's being very sensible."

"Sensible?" she exploded. "He's crazy!" She had to get her mind off Jacobs and back on Whisper before she could talk reasonably again. But Dad was already placing papers in his briefcase, snapping it shut with finality, and slipping into his suit coat before Mattie actually suggested that they buy Whisper.

"Buy her? What use would we have for a Thoroughbred race horse? A disabled one at that?" He checked the clock and patted her hair. "Mattie, be practical."

"But, Dad, I am—really. Hank says we could probably get her for less than five hundred dollars, and she's worth thousands."

That stopped her father for a second. Then, "Five hundred, smive hundred; it makes no sense," he answered with a frown. "I've got to get going, honey. I'll be in late traffic if I stick around another five minutes. See you tonight."

Mattie stood like a stone as she watched Dad disappear out the door. Then disappointment hit her so hard she felt queasy and wrapped her arms tight about her middle. Once Mattie had made her plan for telling Dad her idea, all thoughts of defeat had vanished. She had been so strong in her purpose that she'd forgotten that her family might not want her to have Whisper.

She had failed. Completely. She grabbed the empty cereal box from the table and crumpled it, then rammed it into the wastebasket. Stupid! That's what she was. She couldn't do anything right!

It was so clear to her. Why couldn't Dad see? Whisper needed her. And Mattie needed Whisper.

She heard her mother coming toward the kitchen and rushed out of there without slowing, not until she had closed herself inside the quiet emptiness of the stall.

The dirt floor was cool when she sank down and hugged her knees. Thoughts of the lovely mare tumbled in Mattie's head. Whisper couldn't die! Why hadn't her father understood? What could she have said differently?

Mattie didn't know how long she huddled there. She got up stiffly and gazed out the Dutch door. The spread of fields, the old trees and wild bushes—these were what

Whisper would see if she lived in this barn.

Mattie gripped the top of the door so hard her fingers turned white. Whisper deserved to live here, and that was all there was to it!

Somewhere she would find the right words to convince Dad and Mom. With Saturday so close, though, she would have to try again in the evening.

The day dragged by with Mattie unable to settle at anything. As Dad's arrival time crept nearer, she braced herself to plead her case.

Surprisingly, Dad was the one who spoke first. He began, "Mattie, I saw that look on your face when I left today. I probably should have turned right around and worked this Whisper business out with you, but...." He shrugged. "Well, anyway, I'm sorry."

"It's okay." She'd better let him talk.

He loosened his necktie and pushed off his shoes as he continued. "You caught me off guard. I wasn't expecting you to be wanting a horse now. Any horse."

"I know. I . . ." She couldn't go on. She had done a lousy job of explaining herself.

Mom sat with a magazine open in her lap, obviously listening. "Hey, what's this about?"

"It's about buying the horse Mattie saw yesterday," Dad said.

"My goodness."

"It was only a few days ago that we were all carefully avoiding horse talk for your sake," Dad continued, "and now you've made an about-face."

"And we're glad, Mattie," Mom said.

Mattie nodded, quiet. "I couldn't be that way forever. I feel so much better now that I'm back with horses. They really are important to me, and I'm not going to pretend anymore that I can get along without them."

If Mom and Dad were to understand about Whisper, she was the only one who could make it happen.

Dad seemed to accept what Mattie had said so far. "It just seems you've leaped in a little deep, wanting to own a sick race horse."

Mattie jumped. "You haven't seen her, Dad. She's magnificent. Fantastic! And she's going to be dog food."

Dad scowled and shook his head. Mattie knew he cared about animals, even if it wasn't always practical.

"But we can save her. For a tiny bit of what she is worth, we could buy her, and I could keep her and care for her and love her . . . ."

Dad scratched his cheek thoughtfully. "I have lots of unanswered questions, Mattie. Let me change my clothes, and then we'll talk."

There wasn't a lot more Mattie could say.

Chapter 11

Mattie fidgeted beside her father as he placed the call.

"Mr. Jacobs, my daughter has seen your mare Whisper, and we'd like to make you an offer for her." Dad spoke carefully.

Mattie scowled as Dad held the receiver out slightly so she could hear the answers.

"Whisper's no good to anybody." Jacobs's booming voice leaped from the receiver. "I'm sending her to auction to get the best price I can for dog food. I'm afraid you and your kid are mistaken if you think you can bring that horse back to be worth anything."

"No sir. Mattie . . . we think she's a fine animal and would like to care for her. My daughter is good with horses and could give her some happy years here at our home."

"Sentimentality doesn't impress me, Mr. . . ?"

"Hall. Bob Hall. Then consider this. We'll give you a firm $500 to take her off your hands. From what I've learned of the going prices per pound for horse meat, you'll be lucky to get $350–$400 through the auction." Dad hadn't done his usual careful research, but at least he had asked Hank about auction prices.

Mr. Jacobs hesitated for what seemed like ages and then asked, "How old's your girl? Ten—twelve, I bet. This is no pony we're talking about here. This is a sixteen-hand race horse. How's she going to handle that?"

Dad's doubts blossomed anew on his face. Mattie frowned and shook her head, pleading silently with her father that she could handle Whisper. She knew she was a gentle horse.

But Mr. Jacobs gave no time for anyone to slip in replies. "You'll probably be hustling that horse off to auction yourself." He ended saying, "I'll call it a deal. Come Saturday morning and pick her up. You pay my office man $500. I'm on my way elsewhere."

Dad looked confused, as if he didn't know whether to be upset with the man or happy to have his offer accepted. "Thank . . . thank you," he stammered.

"Just one thing, though, mister," Jacobs growled. "I don't ever want to see that horse on the race track again. You could have her nerves cut—expensive, you probably know—and let her win. You do, and I'll sue. Understand?"

Mattie's father bristled at the threat. "We're not in the racing business. Not even the horse business. We just want..."

"Good!" Jacobs interrupted. "Then see my man Saturday."

Dad looked at the humming receiver, shaking his head. "Nice man," he said quietly.

Mattie hovered close. "But we can have her, can't we?" The words came out on a string of breath.

"We can have her, Mattie. Saturday." Her father still sounded dazed.

"We can have her!" Mattie squealed and flung her arms around him.

Wayne came to see what the uproar was about, his sketching pencil still in his fingers. "What's going on?"

Dropping her fierce grip on Dad's middle, Mattie cried, "I'm getting my horse. This Saturday. And she is so special!" She put her hands up to her face to try to cool her burning cheeks.

"Really?" Wayne's eyes looked huge and bright. "Just like that. All of a sudden you're getting a horse?"

"I can't believe it, but it's true. It's true."

"You can't believe it? I'm overwhelmed!" Dad said. He sat down heavily. "It's just not like me to jump into things. I didn't honestly think we had much chance, and I don't yet know why he decided to sell her to us. Strange man." He shook his head. "Sure hope we're doing the right thing."

"We are!" Mattie cried. "Whisper's a wonderful, beautiful horse. And we're saving her life. Think of that." She also wanted to let her father know how grateful she felt that he had trusted her, taken her judgment that this horse would do for her, but there weren't enough of the right words to say all that.

"I know, honey. You had me convinced of that before I made the call. But you have to admit it's a lot to take on, and I hope you—we"—he quickly corrected himself "are up to it."

Mattie knew Dad was referring to her physical condition. But that simply was not going to be a problem. "Well, it isn't like we're unprepared, Dad. That stall has been waiting a long time. And we've got the pasture."

Mom joined them. "This is like adopting a baby. All at once we are going to have this living being, and we need cereal, formula, and diapers."

"Diapers!" Wayne scoffed.

Mom laughed, and Mattie saw that she was excited, not just putting up roadblocks.

"When're you getting your horse, Mattie?" Wayne wanted to know.

"Saturday," Mom answered for her. "How do we find someone with hay to sell?"

Mattie's stomach tightened for a minute, then she snapped her fingers. "I know. We can ask Gareth's."

"They grow their own hay," Dad said. "But it's still a good idea. They probably know where we can buy some."

"Or just ask Hank; I bet he knows people," Mattie suggested.

"Just ask Hank," Mom said. "It seems Hank is going to become a very important person in our lives."

He already is very important, Mattie thought. He had taken her to Whisper.

"All right," Dad said. "I think we'd better calm down and figure out exactly what has to be done before Saturday." He got a pad and pencil and sat at the kitchen table, motioning the others to join him.

Wayne poured glasses of lemonade for all four and straddled a chair next to Dad.

Mattie had dreamed for such a long time of owning her own horse. Now the dream was really happening! She watched Dad list the jobs to be done.

At midnight Mom pointed to the wall clock. "It's late; time for bed," she reminded.

Emotion had exhausted Mattie, and she crawled into bed willingly. She reached for Tannie Annie and held her under her chin. Stroking the little animal, she murmured, "When I was little, every night I would whisper in your ear my wish for a horse. Maybe that's why I'm getting one named Whisper." She closed her eyes on that thought and slept.

The next few days were full of frantic action. By Friday afternoon a small truckload of bagged wood shavings had been delivered to the Halls' barn, and Mattie and her mother had bought a fifty-pound bag of mixed "sweet" feed. It might take some time to adjust Whisper to her new diet, Mattie thought, so they would order a stock of feed after she'd seen how well Whisper took to this mixture. When Dad helped her empty the feed into two big metal garbage cans where she'd be storing it, she thought it smelled good enough to eat. Molasses and a combination of grains gave off a rich aroma.

Mattie took birthday money she had saved and bought a green corner feeder and a large water bucket to hang on the wall.

At the end of the day, Mattie stood in the doorway of the stall. The bare room had been transformed into a warm, friendly home. Pale yellow shavings lay in a fluffy mat over the floor. The heavy wallboards were spotless and golden. In two corners the feed box and water bucket hung, fresh and bright. There was even a small metal holder for a mineral-salt block.

"Looks pretty good," Wayne observed.

"Nah," Mattie said. "It looks fabulous."

Dad and Mom laughed.

"Whisper's going to love it," Mattie said as she latched the doors and started back to the house with the family.

Mom's arm circled her shoulder. "I'm so glad you're going to get your horse, and I hope you love having it. It's going to mean a lot of hard work, you know."

"I can handle it, Mom," she answered firmly.

Mom squeezed her hand and smiled, but concern still showed in her eyes.

It did bother Mattie the way she ached after the days of getting ready for Whisper. But she certainly wasn't going to mention it. She said, "I'm heading to bed. Hank's going to be here with the trailer at 8:00 sharp, you remember." This was the event she had waited years for. She would be ready.

Chapter 12

"He's coming. He's here!"
Wayne burst into the house. He had been watching the driveway for the first sight of Hank.

"Mom! Dad! Let's go," Mattie called.

It had been agreed that she would ride with Hank in his truck while the rest of the family followed in Dad's car.

Heading back to the highway, Hank said, "Well now, ain't this one beautiful morning?" He dragged out the "beautiful" and winked at Mattie.

In fact, the morning was already hot, with the blank,

milky grey sky of a humid August day. But Mattie agreed with a short "Perfect." She knew Hank was feeling an inside kind of beautiful, just as she was. She and Hank agreed on quite a lot, she had noticed. He had been around checking on things, offering kindly advice the last part of the week, ever since she had gotten in touch to see if he would help them pick up Whisper.

Full of itches and twitches of anticipation, Mattie couldn't join in much small talk. Hank whistled along with songs that tinkled out over the truck radio as he drove.

She could not help glancing back now and then to watch the horse trailer. It was empty now, but Mattie kept thinking that in less than an hour she could look back and know that her own horse was on its way home with her. She closed her eyes and squeezed her hands together, trying to be calm.

It felt as though Jacobs's farm had been moved miles and miles farther away, but at last they entered the gateway and drew to a stop beside the stable.

"You know, Mattie, I would've brought you here that first time without any argument if I'd known it would lead to this. Yes, ma'am, it does my heart good to be a part of what you're doing for that horse," Hank said.

Mattie felt like hugging him. "I really do appreciate your help," she answered.

The family piled out of the car and wasted some minutes admiring the place.

Mattie gave Dad a pleading look. She couldn't do this alone.

Getting the message, he asked, "Where would I find the office, Hank?"

Hank pointed. "It's at the end of the stable—there with

the little white door."

"Come with me, Mattie. You should be in on this."

Mattie turned the knob and stepped in boldly. A small, tidy man looked up at her from behind a tan steel desk.

"Good morning," he said crisply. "Was there someone you wanted to see?"

Her father spoke pleasantly. "Yes, sir, the office man. I'm afraid Mr. Jacobs didn't give me his name."

"That would be me." He reached out a slim hand to shake Dad's. "Samuels is the name."

Dad shook hands with Mr. Samuels and nodded toward her. "I'm Bob Hall, and this is my daughter, Mattie."

Now, Mattie thought. Now that he's heard our name he'll know what to do.

But he merely laid aside his pen and asked, "What can I do for you?"

"Mr. Jacobs said we should pay you our $500, then we could take Whisper," Dad said, and he drew his checkbook from his shirt breast pocket.

"Oh? Whisper? It was my understanding that that horse was being auctioned on the 21st." He tapped his calendar for verification and looked at them. "That's today."

Mattie had gone all tight inside. She cried, "But he said we could buy her today, so she wouldn't have to go!"

The man gave a cluck of disapproval. "It would help if he would let me know," he muttered. He began sifting through a stack of papers and at last drew one out. "Well, I believe here it is. I remember now. This note jotted— would you believe—on the edge of this stock listing. It says '$500/Saturday/Whisper.' I have to be part mind reader to keep this place in the black." He smiled wryly. "I just hadn't figured that one out yet."

Mattie sighed her relief, and Dad stopped frowning. Then, with no further delay or confusion, a check and receipt were exchanged. After all her years of waiting, in two whisks of a pen, Mattie was a horse owner!

The two of them hustled out of the office, eager to find Hank and get Whisper on her way home.

She confided, "Whew! I was scared for a minute! Weren't you?"

Dad grinned down at her and agreed, "It was close, wasn't it? But it worked out." He held out the receipt like a prize to Mattie.

She snatched it and they hurried on to the end of the long stable aisle where they could see Hank talking with a blue-jeaned young man, and Mom and Wayne. Mattie caught a few words.

"No. Wasn't no word. Didn't hear nothing." Then the whole sentence. "Lars's had the order to take that mare today for two-three weeks now. You know that," he said and stuck out his jaw.

Mom saw Mattie and caught her lower lip in her teeth. Wayne stood, silent for once.

The receipt crushed into her fist, Mattie demanded, "What's wrong?"

"Whisper's gone," was the answer. Mattie wasn't sure who had said it, but putting that with what she had heard coming up to them, she knew what had happened.

"What?" Dad exploded.

Then everyone started talking at once.

Mattie broke from the knot of them.

She raced along the path toward the old shed, limping and stumbling as she ran. She had to see for herself. The shed door was open. She halted a moment, then crept into the building. Somehow if she could go about it right, she would find Whisper there, still in the shadows.

Mattie listened as she got used to the darkness, but all she heard was the rasp of her own panting breath. The barn was empty. Whisper was gone. Trying not to cry, she jammed her palms hard against her eyes and took quick gulps of air.

She hadn't heard his steps, but Wayne appeared beside her. He stood a moment, his hands stuffed into his jeans pockets, shifting his weight from one foot to the other. Then he said pleadingly, "You can get another horse, Mattie."

"Shut up!" she raged at him. "I don't want another horse." She dropped her head to her hands again but raised it just as quickly. "Wait a minute. I've got it. We'll go to the auction."

"Huh?" Wayne said.

"Come on, help me." She couldn't run back to the stable; she had run too hard getting here. She would have to use Wayne for support.

Everyone else was standing where she had left them. Mattie started talking before she reached them. "Dad, we've got to go to the auction. We can still buy Whisper."

He groaned. "Mattie, what's the use of talking like that? I don't know a thing about horse auctions. She's probably already sold." He shook his head.

"No! It's early yet. Lars told me all about it, and he said she wouldn't be sold till way late in the day. Dad, there's still a chance." She had hold of his arm, trying to move him.

Dad looked at Mom. She said, "If there's a chance, we should take it, Bob."

"I knew I should never have leaped into this whole affair." But to Mattie's relief, he asked the young man, "Where is this sale?"

"Well, most likely at Buckman's auction barn. That would be Claire, New York," the man answered.

"Most likely," Dad repeated. "But you don't know?"

"Not my job to know. I keep my eyes on things here until Lars gets back from the sale, which I do know he said he was going to."

"Let's ask Mr. Samuels, Dad," Mattie interrupted. "And we've got to hurry."

Her father wasn't fired with the same certainty Mattie was, so she tottered back to the office ahead of him. Her leg was weak and trembling, and she lunged at the door just as Mr. Samuels opened it. She fell against him.

"What the . . . ?" He caught her and pushed her away from him, brushing at his white shirt front as though he feared he had been soiled.

Mattie was shaken by his rebuff and her awkwardness, but Whisper was more important than her pride right then. She straightened herself. "Excuse me," she said. "Where is the auction where Whisper was taken?"

"Are you saying the horse is not here, young lady?"

"No. I mean yes. That's what I'm saying." She was breathing so hard she could barely get words out.

Dad joined her, and they soon determined that the sale was in fact at Buckman's in Claire.

"I'll have to ask for my check back," Dad said.

"Certainly," Mr. Samuels replied. He moved to his desk, opened a drawer with a key he'd drawn from his pocket, then held the retrieved check. He looked at them and said smoothly, "I'll just walk on to the stable with you, if you don't mind." He kept the check in his hand.

Mattie minded. But there wasn't much she could do about it. Impatience was eating at her. But all she could do was watch and keep pushing her hair back from her face as Mr. Samuels took his time talking with the stableman. He even had the gall to check in their horse trailer before he was satisfied they were not trying to make off with his horse without paying for it. Then he returned the check.

Mattie could tell her father didn't like having his word doubted. He tore the check into pieces and dropped them into his shirt pocket. "Let's go, Mattie," was all he said.

Mattie and her father climbed into the car with Mom and Wayne. Hank would follow with the trailer.

"How far is Claire?" Mattie asked from the back seat.

Mom snatched a map from the glove compartment as Dad answered, "Must be two-three hours' drive. I don't know exactly."

Mom looked at Mattie. "Will that be soon enough, honey?" she asked.

"Yes," Mattie answered flatly. But could she really know? She had only Lars's word to go on. What if this sale was not typical? What if they reversed the order and saved the registered stock for afternoon?

Chapter 13

"*T*hree hours!" Wayne complained. "Can't you take me back home first? Me and Brent . . ."

"Wayne, no," Mattie screeched. "There isn't time!"

"Great," he muttered and gnawed at a fingernail.

Mattie huddled in the seat corner, staring out the window, but she saw none of the passing scenery. Her brain was in a flurry as she tried to picture what might be happening at the auction. They had to save Whisper.

And how was Hank getting along? she wondered. They

hadn't seen him on the road. Ohhh, would they all ever get there?

When they reached the edge of Claire at nearly three o'clock, Dad stopped at a gas station for directions to the sale barn. A mile to the east of the small town, they found the sprawling building.

"Sure doesn't look like a barn," Wayne declared.

Mattie had to agree. There was a high center section with single-story wings on each side, strips of board fencing marking outdoor stock pens, and a broad parking lot.

Mattie noted few vehicles in the lot.

"Wow, look at the size of those." Wayne pointed to the long horse trailers beside the sale building. "Wonder how many horses they hold? Lots, I bet."

Mattie's breath caught in her throat. They could belong to the meat buyers. "Are they empty?" she asked shakily.

Wayne scurried for an eager look. "Yep—empty!"

Dad touched her shoulder. "Now that we're here, let's get in and find out what we can do."

"Yes," Mattie agreed, "every minute might count now."

Wayne was already holding open the double glass doors. "Come on, guys," he called.

A long flight of wide steps faced them directly inside. Oh, ouch! Mattie thought. But it was either up them or back out the door, so Mattie struggled ahead as best she could.

At the top of the stairs was a broad walkway, and from there the viewing stands spread out below. The stands formed a semicircle of stepped seats that slanted sharply down, almost to the sawdust-floored arena.

Mattie stood still, taking everything in. A few clusters of people were scattered about the stands. No large, pressing crowd, that was certain, but right then even one person would have seemed a threat to Mattie. The man behind a counter on the far side of the arena talked rapidly into a mike. He was loud, but she could not understand what he said.

Gradually all the sensations sank in, and panic tightened Mattie's throat. How could she know what to do?

Mom touched her and she jumped. "There's an office over here," she said. "We should try that."

A woman in the office leaned on the counter and talked to Mom through an opening in the glass partition. "If you plan to bid, you need a card." She held up a white card with a bold black number printed on it. "And I'll have to see your driver's license, please."

Mom pawed through her purse and laid her license down to be checked. "Can you tell us if a horse named Whisper has been sold yet?"

"No. We have the stock listed by number," she explained casually.

Mom took the bidding card and gave it to Mattie.

Mattie stared at the number 703 while her mother guided her to rejoin Dad and Wayne.

They aimed down an aisle of steps to seats near the ring. Stairs were awkward for her anytime; and these were so big it seemed to Mattie that everyone watched her. She sat, finally, gritting her teeth to keep from shaking.

This is no time to fall apart, Mattie Hall, she told herself. She forced herself to think of what she could do, rather than not do, the way she had learned at the hospital.

She looked up to see a nondescript palomino being

brought into the arena. The man leading her gave her a couple of turns around the ring. Mattie took careful note as the rapid-fire spiel started pouring once more from the auctioneer's mouth.

The big man whacked a gavel on the table once, and his wide-brimmed cowboy hat bobbed. A heavy silver ring flashed as he waved his pudgy hand toward the horse he was selling. He would raise his voice, or lower it, and sometimes briefly pause. But it was nearly impossible for Mattie to make sense of what he was saying.

Soon though, she began to catch the dollar amount the auctioneer was calling for. But even that flew by so fast that at the end Mattie found she had missed a couple of jumps, and the total was higher than she thought he had asked. What if that happened as she bid for Whisper? She might not be quick enough, or understand well enough.

On the edge of her seat, Mattie watched the sale of the next few horses and improved at following the patter. She saw an occasional white card flashed from the stands, but for the most part, the buying was being done by those men standing in the ring, with sawdust on their boots and an easiness about their movements that had kept Mattie from noticing at first that they were even bidding.

Then it struck her. Those men were the meat buyers— the dog food buyers! What's more, the auctioneer was watching them, seldom looking into the stands. More people had left the sale, and it seemed understood that the last horses would go to the meat buyers, just as Lars had said.

Anger steamed through Mattie. Ohh, they couldn't have Whisper! Never!

Dad leaned across Mom and asked, "You all set, Mattie?

You know what to do?"

"I'm ready . . . I think."

"I'll bid for you, if you'd like, Mattie," Mom said and reached for the number card.

"No! I've got to do this."

Mom nodded.

Four more horses were paraded through and dealt with in short order. The auctioneer wasted no time extolling the virtues of those animals, for obvious reasons. They sold anyway—to the meat men.

Mattie moved restlessly in her seat. She felt some pain in her hip, but worry was what kept her wriggling.

"I wish I knew if she's already been sold."

"Maybe you should go down to the pens and check around," Mom suggested. She looked fretful, too.

"I can't," she wailed. "What if she came while I was gone? I'm the only one who knows Whisper." But with her next short breath she said "Whisper" again, for the roan mare had just then limped into the ring. There was Lars, walking Whisper in a tight circle. She looked a hundred times better than any of the other horses. Even unsound, she was still the most gorgeous horse Mattie had ever seen.

Mom had poked Dad, and he asked, "Is that the one?"

Mattie nodded but never lost view of the ring. She concentrated with all her energy. The auctioneer had always thrown out a high figure, gotten no answer, then jumped to a low figure and built up from there. She had to trust he'd do that this time, too.

The men in the ring leaned against the wall, chewed on straw, scratched their beards. This meant nothing special to them. They didn't have to swallow around their hearts the way Mattie did.

The auctioneer banged his gavel and spewed words. Mattie heard 600 clearly. It was all she could do to keep from holding up her card, even though she understood 500 was their absolute limit. She held on for seconds that seemed like hours. As far as she could tell there was no response, and the auctioneer sped on to 325.

Mattie shot her card into the air. The gavel handle was pointed toward a fellow below. He'd beaten her. She had caught the auctioneer's eye, though, and her answering bid to the call for 350 was accepted. She felt as if she were walking a tightrope and dared not be relieved over one safe step; she had to get to the other side.

The bidding moved on frantically. She had no time to tell if others were involved, but to Mattie it was a race between her and that one man. He got the nod at 375, she got it at 400. At 450 he got it again. Then the auctioneer asked 475.

Mattie held her card stiff-armed and waved it. She couldn't see whether her opponent had made a motion. The auctioneer looked around. Then he pointed the gavel at Mattie. "475 once," he called. Pause. "475 twice. Sold to number 703 for four hundred and seventy-five dollars."

Taking great gulps of air, Mattie slumped toward her mother. She must not have breathed through all that bidding. She was thinking clearly, though. She knew Whisper was hers.

Mom was hugging her, saying, "You did it, honey. You did it!"

Dad and Wayne leaped out of their seats and joined in patting her on the back. Dad said, "Let's go get your horse, Mattie." She wondered if her face was beaming as brightly as his right then.

Wayne bounded up the steps two at a time, but for once Mattie didn't envy his agility; it seemed she floated up.

On the concourse she was greeted by a hearty "Let me shake your hand, girl. I'm mighty proud of what you just did."

Hank! My gosh, she'd forgotten all about him. He held out that shovel-sized hand of his to congratulate her. Mattie stuck her hand in his and found she could give a powerful shake, putting all her joy into it.

Dad had gone to pay the cashier, and Wayne shouted at Mattie, "What do we do now?"

"Calm down," she said. She had no idea what to do next.

But as Dad rejoined them Hank said, "Whisper'll be in a stock pen. I'll just run the trailer over, and we'll load her in."

"Sure glad you're here," Dad said. "I've had zero experience trailering horses."

"Glad to be here, Mr. Hall. Just tickled pink." He laughed at himself. "Don't you worry; Whisper's used to being trailered. She won't be any problem loading."

Down at the pen, Lars met them with a grin. "Hank, you were in on this, you old son-of-a-gun."

"Yep. But Mattie's the one that did it. She snatched that mare right out from under the meat ax. Oh." Hank stopped himself. "Folks, I want you to know Lars."

The introduction went on, but Mattie was busy meeting again, and yet for the first time, her horse. Tenderly she put her arms around Whisper's neck.

"Beautiful Whisper," she said softly to the mare. "You're my Whisper now. I'll take care of you."

Chapter 14

Whisper was hers. That was the last thought Mattie had fallen asleep to the night before and the first thought in her head this morning. She couldn't stop smiling.

But as she dressed, her mind took a weird twist. What if it was all a dream? How could something as wonderful as Whisper come to her? Mattie's scalp prickled with thinking it had all happened too fast to be real.

She hobbled through the kitchen without stopping for breakfast and headed straight out to the barn.

Whisper's head appeared over the stall door, with ears pointed and twisting to catch Mattie's noises.

"Oh, Whisper! Hi!" The horse was there, all right. She was real. "And you're mine," Mattie said.

"Did you have a good night, girl?" Mattie talked softly as she stroked the mare's face. "I hope you like your new home. I hope you absolutely love it here," she said. Whisper kept bobbing her head and stretching her neck. "I know, I know. Right now you'd just love to eat. Right?" Mattie had the feeling this horse understood every word she said. When Whisper whickered, Mattie laughed. "So, I have a talking horse!"

She kept her smile as she walked through the barn to the tack room, where she had a bale of hay waiting. Mattie loosened a flake from the bale. For the very first time she was doing this for her horse! Every action carried great meaning on this magical morning.

Mattie stuffed the hay into the feeder, and Whisper turned stiffly and grabbed at it even before Mattie moved away. It was strange to be standing so near that big animal. Sixteen hands was really tall in a small room; nothing about the horse seemed small—or weak, like she was—in that space.

Mr. Jacobs's "This is no pony we're talking about" zipped through Mattie's mind. A shiver stole across her shoulders as she realized Whisper was not just her horse; Whisper was her responsibility.

Mattie sighed. "What do I know about taking care of a horse that hurts all the time?" she asked Whisper. Mattie thought, Just about nothing, that's what. She sagged against the wall and closed her eyes, swamped with doubt.

Mattie had done some reading about navicular disease—

she'd been honest with Hank about that—but it was all vague and full of ifs and buts. Now she had a warm, live animal within arm's reach that depended on her. She listened to the rustling sounds of hay being pulled into Whisper's mouth and great teeth cracking away at the strands. Even Whisper's stomach gurgled. Almost human, Mattie thought. "I'm so stupid. If I were a vet, I'd know what to do for you."

A vet. Of course! Mattie popped back away from the wall. She'd been making worries instead of taking action. Well, no more! Funny how every time she felt hopeless, her recovery from the accident helped her, at the very least reminded her that moaning got nothing done.

Now she would get Whisper her morning grain; that was something she could do. Then a bit later she would give the mare a good grooming and keep her bedding clean; that was something else she could do.

Mattie went back to the house, ready to find a vet for Whisper.

As she pulled open the kitchen screen door, Mom held the phone receiver out to her. "For you. It's Hank."

Mattie reached for it but clapped her hand over the mouthpiece as Wayne jostled past her.

"How's Whisper?" he asked. "I'm gonna see her," he said, already half out the door.

"But don't you do anything," Mattie called. Who said she wanted to share her horse with him? Then she remembered the phone in her hand.

It was easy to share Whisper with Hank. He had some rights to her. Mattie learned the name of a good equine vet in their area. She made a note of the name, Dr. Klamson, and thought to ask Hank if he would like to come over when the vet made his visit.

"If it doesn't interfere with your family, I mean," she apologized. She had made demands on Hank's time before without thinking he might be needed at home.

"No, ma'am, that's no problem. Lost my wife a couple years back, and we never had young'uns. I'll bring my old bones right over whenever you say the word."

"Thanks," she said. "I'll call you when I know the time."

An idea came to Mattie as she hung up. Maybe Hank didn't always feel as cheerful as he seemed. It could be an act to cover up a big loneliness. She shrugged, thinking she had better get on to calling the vet for an appointment. First she'd have to check with Mom and Dad.

Two days later, at nine in the morning, Dr. Klamson came. Hank had pulled in a few minutes before him. Mattie was grateful the doctor hadn't kept her waiting any longer. She had been having trouble sleeping, fretting about how to help Whisper.

The vet began a careful examination of the horse. Mattie's shoulders stayed tense as she waited to hear his verdict.

Dr. Klamson later straightened from bending over Whisper's front hoof. His gentle hands moved across the mare's shoulder as he told Mattie, "I checked the original x-rays with Dr. Ross; he's the one who first diagnosed your mare's problem. They show that the navicular bone had definite changes from normal. All of the tests I've done here this morning confirm that." He gave Mattie a soft look. "Everything points to navicular disease."

Hank sighed. Had he expected something better? Mattie wondered. Something curable? She hadn't. Well, maybe she had done a little wishing—wishing that this vet would contradict the first, and that Whisper would soon be gloriously fit. But that hadn't lasted long. Mattie knew wishing gained her nothing, no matter how tempting it was. It hadn't undone her injuries, and it wouldn't undo Whisper's.

"What can I do," she asked, "so she doesn't hurt so much?"

Dr. Klamson seemed relieved by her reaction. He probably had thought she would go all weepy or something. "Let's put her inside now, and we can have a good talk about your options," he answered.

Hank reached for the lead. "I'll take her for you, Doc. Little Whisper and me are going to be great friends. Ain't that right, girl?" He spoke to the mare as he led her back to the stall.

Mattie and the doctor settled on the antique bench Dad kept beside the barn. He called it his whittling bench, but she'd never seen him do more than sit there in the sun with a book. Dr. Klamson took a pad and pen from his coverall pocket. He had her total attention.

"Now, the way you manage your horse can make some difference in how comfortable she will be day to day. You want to help her keep weight off her front heels. So, first, get a load of dirt and build a mound near the middle of your stall. That way when she stands watching out the door..."

"She'll do that a lot," Mattie inserted. She felt warm and good when he referred to Whisper as her horse.

"Yes." He smiled patiently. "When she stands watching, her front end will slant slightly downward so she rests more on her toes than on her heels. Understand?"

Mattie nodded. "Yeah."

"It's good that you have a dirt floor rather than concrete so you can make that change, plus it will be easier on her feet anyway."

Mattie was glad she had taken a lot of thought deciding which kind of floor to have in her stall back when Dad and she were planning.

"Next, see that your farrier is here at least every six weeks. He should keep the hooves trimmed with a short toe, long heel, and you can ask for special eggbar shoes to help keep the weight off those heels." The vet noted that as step two on his pad.

Mattie fretted to herself: farrier? How do I find a farrier? That was one thing she had not thought of. Maybe Hank would know whom Gareth's used. She had seen someone there shoeing the lesson horses a few times.

"Then, always remember that a big part of the pain with navicular disease comes from poor circulation of blood to that area. So being confined won't be good for your mare."

"Oh." This was a new, alarming idea to Mattie. "You mean she's going to be worse if she isn't ridden?" She did not want to have to say "I can't ride."

"No, no." He waved his hand as if to wipe away that suggestion. "Hard work is not good, either. What she needs is to be able to ramble about, to keep a bit active."

"I can put her in the pasture every day."

"Yes, that's the idea. You'll find her stiff and sore-acting in the mornings, but she should loosen up some with easy activity." Dr. Klamson stretched his legs and scratched one dark and wiry eyebrow. "Otherwise, do all the things you would normally do for a horse to keep her healthy:

good daily grooming, clean bedding, regular worming, adequate feed. It looks as if she's been underfed by her former owner, but don't get her heavy." He looked directly at Mattie, still with calm concern. "Do you have any questions?"

No, she had no questions. But she couldn't stop a sigh. Her head began to feel weary. Everything sounded huge and terribly important now.

"And last . . ."—Mattie's shoulders slumped at the thought of anything more—". . . I'm going to prescribe bute daily. It's a painkiller, a little like our taking aspirin. Won't cure her, but it will make her feel better for a time." He smiled.

Mattie looked down. She knew her discouragement was showing. She had been so sure she could take care of Whisper, and now the job loomed large before her.

Dr. Klamson roused himself and visited his truck while Mattie sat mulling over his instructions. He returned with a month's supply of bute. She had known of the medicine, and she thought it a good idea for horses to have their own pain drug, but now she wondered how much it cost. Dr. Klamson gave her a bill for the examination and bute. She'd work it out later with Dad as to how much the medicine would cost each month.

Mattie watched the vet leave, absentmindedly pressing a hand to the ache in her back. Then she squared her shoulders and headed to the stall. Whisper reached her finely sculptured head toward her, and Mattie told herself, I've fought hard before; I can do it again.

Chapter 15

*H*aving a horse filled a huge hole in her life. Mattie had done everything Dr. Klamson said, and it gave her deep-down pleasure seeing Whisper improve. The bute treatment kept her comfortable, her coat was silky shiny, and she was already filling out over her ribs.

But summer was coming to an end; school was due to start again soon. Mattie began to think about the other hole in her life, the one she'd hidden away all summer long, just as she'd once stuffed away her horse things. She missed Jill.

Wayne had bounced around with Brent and other buddies all July and August. Mattie had pretended friends didn't matter.

She lay now on her bed, one hand on the phone. Should she? She agonized. Could she? Jill had not called her after the time Mattie hung up on her. Well, no, that wasn't true. Jill had called once, but Mattie had told Wayne to say she wasn't able to talk. So now it was up to Mattie.

She punched in the number. Maybe she won't answer; maybe she won't be home.

"Hello." Jill's familiar voice.

Mattie hesitated.

"Hello?" Jill repeated.

"Jill—hi," Mattie finally got out.

"Mattie. . . Mattie? That you?"

"It's me." She breathed easier. "What've you been up to?"

"Not much; summer's been a real drag." There was a space where Mattie imagined Jill deciding if she was worth talking to. "Hey, I heard you got a horse."

"Yeah . . . I did."

"That's super!"

"You think so?" Mattie had not planned to mention Whisper at first, so she wouldn't put Jill off, and now here Jill was sounding thrilled about it.

"Sure! It's what you always wanted." Jill was beginning to talk just as easily as they used to. Mattie rolled onto her back and relaxed.

She dared to ask, "Could you come over someday soon? I want you to see my horse more than anything. Do you forgive me?"

Jill's laugh rippled. "Yes, and yes! And do you forgive

me, too? We've got tons to talk about. And I really want to see your horse—just not get too close to it, you know. You won't expect me to get on it, will you?"

"Her, not it, Jill. Her name's Whisper, and no, I'm not quite that crazy yet."

The next thing Mattie knew, she had passed an hour talking with Jill. Mattie had an appointment the next day back at Mercy Central for a checkup, then Mom was taking her shopping for school clothes. Jill had to go to her uncle's cottage on Tupper Lake for the weekend, so it was decided Monday was the day she would visit Mattie.

Monday. Mattie thought maybe she could even help Jill get over being afraid of horses. If not, that was okay, too.

"I wanted to be better before school," Mattie grumbled as she tried on new jeans.

"Honey, you are better," Mom protested. "You heard the doctor. You're progressing very well..."

"I mean look better. Look better, Mom." These days she had to explain things to Mom, it seemed.

Her mother grimaced, but she didn't argue the point.

Actually, Mattie thought, turning slowly in front of the fitting room mirror, in some ways she did look better than last year. If only she didn't have to move.

She tugged the jeans off. At least her mother let her get tight ones. "These will be fine, Mom." She dressed, thinking back to some of the barbs she had taken last spring, beginning with "Tarzana" and on to "fish-hips," and even worse. But she was stronger now and could go longer before aching, and her hard work at exercising had helped some, she thought. She stared in the mirror, picturing her nerves zapping messages from her brain to her muscles. When would they zap away the limp?

As Mattie combed her hair, bleached the lightest blond by summer sun, she thought of Ben. Maybe this year they would be in some of the same classes. She hoped so. Ben had been at least twenty minutes' worth of the conversation with Jill, and Jill didn't even know him. Yet.

The next day Whisper whickered a welcome.

"Hi, girl, how you doing?" Mattie answered. She scratched Whisper's head and straightened the silky forelock with her fingers.

Whisper snuffed at Mattie's pockets. "You're doing great, that's how you're doing," Mattie pronounced. Inside she felt she was doing okay, too. Whisper was better because of her.

Mattie unlatched the stall door. "Out you go now," she said. "Get a little exercise, girl." With the stall empty, Mattie forked wet shavings into a wheelbarrow. Wayne would empty it for her. It stung her pride to still need help. Someday, she kept telling herself, she would do it all!

Wiping sweat from her upper lip, Mattie put the pitchfork back in the tack room and walked into Dad's part of the barn. It was cooler there than outside. She might as well rest a minute, she thought, and started to lean against a barrel. But she stopped. Probably that barrel had been there for ages, but she hadn't given it a thought. It was on its side, raised off the floor about waist high on a wooden brace. There was a spigot at one end and telltale blobs of oil her father used for the cars and tractor.

That barrel was shaped a lot like the midsection of a horse. Yes, just like a horse. Mattie snatched an empty feed bag from the floor, spread it over the cool metal, and, before she could change her mind, tried to straddle the barrel.

Her knee clunked with a dull thud against the metal. She took her leg in her hands and tried lifting it higher. "Oops!" She laughed at herself. The barrel was farther up than she had figured.

If at first you don't succeed . . ., Mattie thought, and she looked around. She spied an old wooden crate in a corner. That might work. Setting it upside down, she stepped up, then half flung, half yanked her right leg over. Success! "Yahoo!" Mattie yelled, a wild cowpoke for an instant.

Then she clamped her mouth shut and took some quick breaths. None of her exercises had stretched her laterally so hard. It hurt. Right then she was glad she was not on a real live horse. At least this thing wasn't going to bounce her up and down. Mattie gave a few test squeezes against the side of her pretend horse. Very feeble squeezes they were. A real horse wouldn't go any more than this thing will with that touch, she told herself.

Just then she heard Wayne scuffing his feet in the gravel, and Hank whistling one of his tunes. No sense in trying to hurry off the barrel; Mattie wasn't even sure she could get off. She crossed her fingers that the guys might go on to the stall without seeing her.

Not a chance! Wayne caught sight of her right away. "Hey, whatja doing?"

Hank chortled. "Well, will you look at that girl." The pure pleasure in his face kept Mattie's anger down. But she didn't enjoy being discovered.

"What's it look like I'm doing?" she flung back.

"Riding a crazy horse," Wayne said matter-of-factly.

Mattie grinned despite herself. "Just seeing what it might feel like."

Wayne stuck his fists on his hips. "Well, you aren't

going to ride Whisper."

She pulled the ends of her mouth down and batted her eyelids at him. "I know I'm not going to ride Whisper." Anyway, what made him Whisper's big brave protector all of a sudden?

Hank never let them spat long. "Come on, Wayne," he said. "Let's see if we can help Mattie off of this contraption. You ready to dismount?" he asked her.

"I have to be able to get on and off myself... but I'll take your help this time."

"This time?" Hank asked.

"Yep. I'm going to ride this every day." It seemed a perfect plan to Mattie. If she kept using the right muscles, the right way, well...

"Okay. We'll see to it that you've got something solid for clambering up here."

So Hank and Wayne built steps with a handrail, and Mattie rode her barrel horse every day. Now that she was stronger, Vince said she could do a stair exercise, too. So she would stand with her toes on the step and raise and lower her heels. Maybe someday she actually could hold her heels down hard in good hunt seat position. Posting trot? She wondered. Last year it had been so natural that her post had been almost a reflex, but how could she get her body to do it now?

Fall days edged into weeks until two months had passed. School had always been most fun early in the year, when it was great to be back with all the kids, and before certain classes or certain teachers became tiresome. Mattie was glad this fall was the same. Ben showed up in her lunch period. At least that meant they could talk.

Mattie was busy. Now she had to fit in all of her time

with Whisper around school, plus her own exercises. At least she didn't have to go back to physical therapy regularly. She didn't really miss Vince. He had been very important to her recovery, but, still, she found him easy to put behind her. Janice, on the other hand, she wished she could see once in a while. Old guts and grit, Mattie would think, and smile to herself.

Saturdays belonged mostly to Whisper. One Saturday afternoon Mattie and her mother made a trip to a tack shop. As she picked up more salt blocks for Whisper, Mom said, "I'm happy you only want one horse, Mattie. Whisper is a dear, dear animal. But, you know, she is dear in another sense of the word, too."

Sure she knew. And she was concerned about the money. Mattie smiled sheepishly at Mom, who wrinkled her nose at her as if to say don't worry.

Then while her mother waited at the counter for the clerk to figure their bill, Mattie scanned the magazine rack. The display caught her eye with a bold lead article in the current issue of a popular horse magazine.

Mattie grabbed it. "Mom. Look! Navicular disease! I really need to find out more."

Mom could never resist a good magazine anyway, so she added it to their pile on the counter.

As soon as they got home, Mattie went out to the pasture, her shoes crunching brown leaves as she walked. The air had a cool edge to it. Mattie clutched her magazine to her sweater for warmth as she leaned into the board fence to look for Whisper. There she was, grazing at the far side of the open field. Only two trees dotted the space, one huge old black walnut and a skinny scrub tree—just enough to offer protection when Whisper wanted it.

Mattie never could whistle and Wayne had given up showing her how, but Whisper would come to the sound of her name. Mattie cupped her hand to her mouth and called, "Whiissperr!"

The mare's neck shot upright. She stopped nibbling, alert now.

Reaching her hand out over the fence, Mattie called again. Whisper walked a few paces and then suddenly kicked into a gallop. She raced the length of the field to Mattie. What a sight! Her shiny body stretched out in a natural and free expression of grace and speed, and her gleaming mane and tail flashed. Mattie felt her chest could barely hold the swelling of her heart as she watched her Whisper. Only once before had she seen her run, take off like a kid out of school. Usually she was too sore and stiff from favoring her bad feet—even with bute.

Whisper slowed and stopped. She gave Mattie's empty hand a hopeful lick, so Mattie reached down for a tuft of grass. "Here's something for you, you beautiful lady." Mattie patted her neck and murmured to her till Whisper pulled away, still frisky. "Okay, go on. I'll give you another hour out here, then it's back to the stall."

She laughed and thought, I sound just like Mom. She felt like a mom, too, loving Whisper so much and being so proud of her. She hurried back to the house then to close herself in her room, where she could devour the magazine article she still carried with her.

Chapter 16

"**I**socks? What? I can't even say it, girl, and I sure enough never heard of it," Hank answered. Mattie had dialed him as soon as she had finished her reading.

"Isoxsuprine," Mattie repeated. She twisted and untwisted the phone cord. "I hadn't heard of it either, but I just read a great article about navicular disease that told about it." Her voice was shrill with excitement.

"Well, you're way ahead of me, Mattie. Never was much of a reader."

Oh, please listen, she thought. She needed to get it all out—now! "It says that some horses with navicular disease are being helped with this new drug, isoxsuprine hydrochloride. I memorized the name as soon as I saw it might be the answer for Whisper, and I wanted to ask you about it right away."

"That so, huh? Well, I never heard tell of it. You know, Mattie, I would have told you anything I knew that might cure Whisper."

Mattie nodded. "I guess this is something new. I wonder if Dr. Klamson knows about it?"

"Sounds like you ought to talk to him."

That's what she wanted to hear, a little encouragement for the next step. But for now she had more to tell, and the words tumbled out. "The main thing it does is increase the circulation of blood. The article says only ten percent of the horses tested didn't change with the drug. The largest group of horses were sound after just three weeks."

"Whooee!" Hank gave a hoot that hurt her ear. "Three weeks. Wouldn't that be great for Whisper?"

"I know, but we'd better not get our hopes up until we see what I can find out."

Mom and Dad were more cautious than Hank. She had expected that, but when she explained her new information to them fully, they agreed Mattie should try to learn more.

Her parents insisted she wait until Monday after school to contact Dr. Klamson, because a vet should be called on Sunday only if it's an emergency. Well, this felt like a purebred emergency to Mattie! By Monday, she might as well have stayed home from school for all the attention she gave it. But at last she could make her call.

Luckily Dr. Klamson was in his office after finishing his day's visits. She posed her question to him. "Dr. Klamson, what can you tell me about isoxsuprine hydrochloride?"

Mattie couldn't keep the disappointment out of her voice when she found he knew little more than she did. He was aware of the drug but had never used it. In fact, Whisper was the first navicular horse he'd treated for quite some time. He did suggest the names of three vets who might be able to help her, so she perked up and gave him a hearty "Thank you, doctor."

"Good luck, and let's keep in touch about this. Okay?" Dr. Klamson said before hanging up.

Mattie rehearsed what she would ask before calling any of the other vets. Still, she had to choke the receiver to keep it from slipping through her nerve-sweaty hand. She had spoken to the first two people and was on strike three, she thought, when she finally began to get answers.

Dr. Catherine Dade was last on her list but first to be of help when Mattie got through to her.

"It's hard to say how effective isoxsuprine is, or to even know for sure what exactly it does," the friendly woman said. "We don't get that many navicular horses, but we did treat one this past year."

"You used isoxsuprine?"

"Yes. But we used all the other standard treatments too, you see, and got good results."

"Uh-huh," Mattie answered. She guessed that meant they couldn't tell what had helped the horse most.

"As far as I know, the University is doing the most to test the drug," Dr. Dade added. "There'll come a day when we know a lot more about it."

Mattie scowled. She couldn't wait for "a day." "Does

102

isoxsuprine hurt the horse?'' The article had sounded so positive. She couldn't believe it wouldn't help.

"Most likely not. Certainly not that I have seen. Do you want to try it on a horse of your own?" Dr. Dade sounded keenly interested.

"Yes." Mattie couldn't say more.

"Well, have your own vet call me, and if he agrees to go ahead, I'll see that he gets a supply of the drug, and he can monitor the treatment."

Mattie felt dizzy with relief. She had made so many phone calls, three of them to total strangers, and she had gotten what she wanted! She sat down at the kitchen table, gulped a glass of water, and explained everything to Mom and Dad before she phoned Dr. Klamson again. She felt sure that he would go along with her on this.

Dr. Klamson was willing, but it was four long days before Mattie heard from him again. The achingly slow hours of waiting paid off when he brought her the first bottle of isoxsuprine hydrochloride.

A big name for such little pills, Mattie thought happily as she set about mashing them. Dr. Klamson had left her with the instruction to mash twelve of the tablets twice a day for Whisper.

"Want a hand with that, gal?" Hank asked, pressing close.

"No, thanks," she answered without stopping. "I'm getting there. Only a few more to mash."

Wayne was hanging around nearby. "How come you have to pound those pills up like that, anyway?" he asked.

"Because, that's why!" But she couldn't stay curt. "Because the vet says that's the easiest way for a horse to take this medicine."

Hank commented wryly, "Well, let's hope maybe Whisper decides to take hers whole. Smashing a dozen aspirin-sized pills twice a day is going to get old mighty fast."

"Oh, I can do it," Mattie said and pounded a little harder. "Just as long as it helps Whisper."

Hank patted her shoulder, and Mattie looked up from her work to smile.

Whisper took the medicine along with her sweet feed without complaint. She licked with her broad tongue around the edges of her feeder as usual. Mattie felt as satisfied as Whisper must have, watching her in her ritual—the licking, the half closing of her lids with the long eyelashes in a declaration of bliss. She stroked the teddy bear softness of the mare's shaggy winter coat. It was no doubt the first winter she had been allowed to keep such a cozy coat. But it was necessary, since she wasn't being worked and spent a lot of hours outside.

Mattie latched Whisper's stall door, then gave a gentle squeeze to Hank's arm through his heavy denim coat sleeve. "Come in with me," she said. "You know by now that Mom always has a pot of coffee."

He laughed. "Yep! I have to admit I'm growing right partial to your mother's coffee."

And over their cups of coffee Mrs. Hall invited Hank to join the family for Thanksgiving dinner next week. Mattie had never seen a burly old man look so much like a kid who'd just opened the one present he'd been desperately hoping for.

After three weeks of treatment with the little white pills, Mattie stopped the daily bute dose for Whisper.

"Watch her, Dad. She's moving better, don't you think?" She squinted her eyes in concentration. Flecks of snow sprinkled the air, and her cheeks tingled, but Mattie could have stood there at the fence watching Whisper for hours.

Dad was intent, too. "It's hard to tell, Mattie. I'd say better, yes. But I'm not a very good judge, you know." He wanted it to be better, like she did, Mattie could tell.

They watched awhile, then strolled toward the house, neither in a hurry in spite of the chill. Mattie walked fairly evenly, and Dad suddenly squeezed her sideways against his solid chest. "You're better, too, Mattie. You know that?"

She lowered her head and couldn't answer. Mattie was sure she was improving all the time, but it was great to hear her father say so. His notice made it more than just something in her mind. She let him keep his arm around her till they reached the kitchen door and the delicious smell of doughnuts frying tickled Mattie's nose. Mom made those doughnuts when winter set in, just as surely as geese flew south.

By the time the Thanksgiving and Christmas holidays had departed, having filled the Hall house with the warmth and fun of giddy get-togethers, Mattie's supply of isoxsuprine was gone. And now she was positive.

Chapter 17

"**M**om, it works. It really works!" She landed in a kitchen chair after having bedded Whisper for the night.

"What works, honey?" Mom shoved a sudsy dishcloth around the counter.

Mattie frowned. Her head ached, and she wished her mother would stop and listen for a minute. "The medicine, the isoxsuprine. I can hardly believe it. But Whisper acts like a new horse. You should see her scramble around out there, through the snow and all." She knew it wasn't likely her mother would spend any time outside watching Whisper cavort. She was the family hothouse plant in the winter. Anyway, Mattie had certainly kept her aware of any slight improvement the mare had shown.

Mom wiped her hands and went to Mattie. "I'm so glad, honey. She's a lucky horse to have you." With a hug she pressed her cheek to Mattie's forehead. "Hey, you feel hot." She peered at Mattie. "Do you have a fever?"

Mattie shrugged and gave Mom a dismal look. Her head felt leaden, and she was fighting the urge to lay it on her arms right there on the kitchen table.

"Oh, Mattie, you're sick. Come on, let's find the thermometer."

Mattie didn't resist, and as she trailed along toward her bedroom, the knot she had felt in her stomach all the while she'd been working with Whisper suddenly rose to her throat. She made a fast detour to the bathroom. How she detested throwing up! It left her so weak-kneed and trembly Mom had to help her to bed.

"You poor thing." Mom tucked the soft blue blanket around her neck. "Looks like you've caught the flu that's going around. Sleep now. I'll be checking on you."

Mattie longed to sleep but rested only fitfully that entire night. Twice more she made the stumbling trek to the bathroom and back to bed.

It must have been around four in the morning when she first heard it. She was sure it had been raining, droning away heavily in the background, but suddenly it sounded like someone throwing corn kernels at the window, a pecking, rattling racket that came with each thrust of a strong wind. She reached to her radio on the nightstand and turned it on low. The constancy of the music helped cover the intruding noises, and she dozed again.

"Hey, Mattie, school's canceled." Wayne had flung her door open and stood calling to her from the hallway. At least he was smart enough not to get too near her germs.

"Huh?" she answered foggily. Sure school was canceled for her. She was sick.

"Look outside," he urged. But he couldn't wait for her to look. "We had an ice storm last night." His eyes were sparkling. "Everything's slick as slime."

"Okay. Just leave." She didn't try raising her head until he'd yanked her door closed. But then she saw that the outdoor world had become a fantasy. She would be excited, too, if she didn't feel so awful.

Sunlight glistened from humps and hillocks of snow that looked smoothly sealed in plastic wrap. It bounced off trees, ice-coated down to the last twig.

Mattie collapsed against her pillows. "Wow," she said. But by then she felt dizzy even lying and was glad to see Mom come in to help her.

The flu had taken firm hold, and it was three days more before the worst was over. Mattie had hated doing it, but she asked Wayne to care for Whisper. She knew he could do all that was needed, but she felt guilty about deserting her horse. Too weak to be up, Mattie passed the time in her own bed and on the family room sofa, where she could watch TV.

Wayne missed only one day of school. It didn't take long for road crews to clear away highway ice around there with salt and sand, but the fields and pathways remained covered and treacherous. Whisper had to be kept in.

"How is she doing, Wayne?" Mattie asked, not for the first time. "It's driving me nuts not being able to see her."

"Don't worry. I think she's okay." He looked uncertain.

"What do you mean, you think?" Mattie tried not to sound challenging.

Wayne shook his head. "She's getting restless, I guess, from being in so much. When I groomed her, she kept standing on first one foot, then the other, like maybe she was bored."

Mattie frowned. Bored? Or hurting?

The next day Mattie asked Wayne the second he got home from school, "Will you go out and check Whisper for me?"

"Just a minute." He was agreeable enough but had to ruffle Flossy's hair and grab a handful of cookies first.

Wayne was back in the house shortly. "Mattie, she's lying down. And she doesn't want to get up." The rasp of fear rang in her ears.

"I'm coming."

She knew it! She knew things were going wrong for Whisper. She was maddeningly slow-moving, trying to stuff herself into a parka, her mittens, tall boots. She still had a disconnected feeling, as if she weren't really one with her body. It was a good thing Mom was out buying groceries; she'd never let her past the door.

The two of them crept to the barn by way of the driveway in one of Dad's tire tracks. Mattie hunched along behind Wayne. Dad had managed to clear the drive enough to get in and out to work. Everything else remained locked in frozen covers; the frigid air held.

Whisper was still stretched out when Wayne opened the stall door, but she lifted her head. Mattie felt flooded with guilt, seeing her horse down, and was seized with a fit of shivers. "Whisper!" she cried. The mare crooked her legs under her and rolled to her stomach. The usual swift movement that brought her upright did not follow.

"Come on, Whisper," Mattie begged.

With a grunt close to a groan, Whisper heaved herself up. Mattie squeezed the broad neck between her arms. The mare gently bumped at Mattie with her forehead and then pulled away to stand, head lowered. She pointed first one front foot, then the other.

"Oh, poor Whisper. What am I going to do for you?" Mattie couldn't think clearly; she could only feel sorry for Whisper and for herself.

"We still have bute," Wayne broke in. "Want me to give her a dose?"

Of course! "Yes. That's what we'll do." She plodded to the cabinet in the tack room where she kept the bute, mad at herself for not beating Wayne to that idea.

They gave Whisper the pain killer along with a treat of sweet feed and turned to leave while Whisper munched away. At least she was willing to stand long enough to eat.

Mattie noticed the fresh bedding. "Hey! It looks good in here. You've been keeping it clean."

"Sure." He pointed as he latched the stall door. "I put those boards down to make it easier to get over to the manure pile. Tricky in this ice."

Mattie had not been up for a long time since getting sick. Stumbling, she grabbed Wayne's coat.

He halted until she was ready to walk again. "Just keep hanging on. I don't mind," he said.

Wayne can be so nice sometimes, she thought. She kept her hold.

Bed felt lousy to Mattie that night. She had been in it

too much. Unable to keep her eyes closed, she traveled the length of walls that were lighted by the clear night, stopping on the horse calendar. Her new Christmas calendar was due to be turned to the next month soon. *Where have I gotten in a year?*—*almost a whole year?* she thought. *This was so much like lying in that hospital bed. It had been icy outside then, too. It's hopeless,* she whined to herself. *The pain isn't gone. Every time I do half of what I want to do, it's back again. When will I walk the way I used to? When will I ride again?*

Almost against her will Mattie's eyes slipped on toward the horse poster. *And now Whisper is right back where she was in the beginning. I haven't done her any good.*

Mattie squeezed her eyes shut to try to stop it, but she could feel little drips begin at the inner corners. She swiped at the tears, but there was no fighting them this time. She stuck her head under her pillow to keep anyone from hearing and gave in to all the hurts and defeats she had tried to bury. Guttural sounds pushed up into her throat, choking her until she sobbed them out.

Finally, hoarse and hiccuppy, she was through with crying. She shoved aside her pillow, blew her nose, and barely rolled onto her back before dropping to sleep.

Grandma had once said crying is good for you. Mattie had questioned it then, but now she was a believer. A whole lot of self-doubt had been washed right out of her, and this morning she felt well enough to join the family for breakfast for the first time since she'd been sick.

"Look at that sunshine," Dad said, making a grand gesture with his English muffin. "They say a warm front's coming through. Maybe we'll finally get rid of this ice."

"I hope so," Mattie said. "I've got to get Whisper out

to exercise. She's lame again, Dad."

Her father nodded. "Wayne was telling me. I'm sorry."

"Yeah," Mattie answered and stirred her cereal. She was sorry, too. But today she didn't feel hopeless about it. "I think she's going to keep needing isoxsuprine, Dad."

He looked at her and then into his coffee cup before taking a slow sip. "Well. . . see how she is after you've had her in pasture for a while. She may just be stiffened up, more than in pain." He added, "It's too bad that stuff is so expensive."

Mattie took up her spoon again. The hot cinnamon oatmeal tasted like a feast to her. Dad might be right; she would wait to see if Whisper improved with exercise.

Over the weekend the ice melted. Dozens of rivulets poured down the steep roof of the barn, and solid snowbanks turned squishy. Then early in the week a new fall of fresh, feathery snow came.

Mattie was able to return to school and spent extra hours each evening making up missed studies. That didn't keep her from a determined vigil over Whisper's reaction to pasture freedom. The result was what she had expected and dreaded, not what she had hoped. At the end of the week she placed an order for more isoxsuprine.

Chapter 18

*E*very day Mattie's school bus route took her past a small, aged lesson stable called Day Farms. Usually she avoided looking that way, since it was a depressing place. But all week now she had swiveled her head to study it, deciding gradually if she could stand to do it. Then she went to her mother.

"Mom. I'm going to get an after-school job."

"Oh, Mattie. You're doing so much already, trying to keep your grades up and care for Whisper and . . . ." She folded her arms and leaned against the doorjamb. "Why do you want a job?" she asked quietly.

"To help pay for Whisper's medicine." Mattie raised her chin a bit. "I want her to have it as long as she needs it."

"I know you do, honey, and she will. We'll manage. I hate to see you take on any more while you're still healing." Mom's frown lines deepened.

"She's my horse, Mom. I can help." Mom's arguments were exactly what she had expected, but she wasn't going to lose.

"Well... if you think you can find a suitable job..."

"I'm positive I can. You know Day Farms over on Quaker Road? Old Mrs. Day is always hiring kids to clean stalls and stuff. You don't have to be sixteen or anything, and it's work I know how to do."

"It's hard work, Mattie! And that's not a very nice place. We didn't want your riding lessons there, even though it's just around the corner."

Her mother wasn't giving in yet, Mattie saw. "I know all that, Mom, but I can handle it. I can do more than you think I can."

"I think you can do pretty much what you put your mind to, Mattie." Mom reached to hold Mattie's hands in hers and smoothed the backs with her thumbs. "You'll quit if it makes you hurt."

Mattie nodded, then grabbed her mother in a tight hug.

Getting hired at Day Farms was simple; Mrs. Day usually needed help, since no one stayed with her very long. She was positively ancient, and Mattie thought she had long forgotten how to treat horses—or people, for that matter— but Mattie was set on doing a good job.

At the end of her first week at Day Farms, Mattie ached all over. She had used her good muscles twice as hard, she guessed, to make up for the weak ones, because now everything hurt! "Rats!" she said and dragged herself away from the stall. She had wanted to be out waiting for her mother. She pumped up her last drips of energy and made it to the car.

Mattie felt Mom's eagle eyes going over her before she backed out of the parking lot. "How do you feel?" she asked, watching the road.

"Fine." Mattie couldn't look at her mother.

"Mattie..." Mom said in a warning tone.

"Mom, I'm not quitting!" Mattie exploded.

"I thought we had an agreement," her mother answered.

"It'll get easier, Mom. I'll get used to it." Mattie felt rotten not keeping her word to Mom. But she knew she was right about this. Well... she hoped she was right—that it would get better. Whisper needed her.

Mattie gave up evening television and went to bed early for a few weeks. And she had been right! She was getting stronger all the time. Plus—and this was the best—Whisper felt good once again. Dr. Klamson hadn't found any bad side effects from the special medicine so far, and the mare was a lot more comfortable than before.

After a month of working every day after school, Mattie told her mother, "I'm cutting back a little, Mom. Mrs. Day says it's all right if I go just three afternoons now."

"Good." Mom sounded surprised but was smiling.

"Well, I figured now I know I can do it, you know I can do it, so why overdo it?" Mattie laughed with her mother. This way Mom would be less worried for her, and she would still be helping with expenses.

A council with her father had helped Mattie make up her

mind, too. Dad pointed out that even though there were big costs with Whisper, they were partly balanced by some credits. "You don't cost me a weekly riding lesson," he said, "or show fees."

"And I don't need a new hunt coat and breeches every time I grow some more," Mattie added.

"And you don't need a saddle and bridle—those things can really run high," he finished.

And so the job issue had been settled.

That same night, Mattie's parents hosted a St. Patrick's Day party, as they did most years. It had to do with celebrating the Irish blood in Mom's family, but mainly, Mattie thought, it was just an excuse for a good time.

As the evening waned, Mattie took a last shamrock cookie and her mug of hot cider to her room. Down the hall she could still hear Hank's bass and Wayne's tenor voices above all the others. Didn't Wayne know it was time for him to get to bed? Oh, well.

She snuggled into bed and then opened a tack catalogue that had come in the mail. Guess once you were on their mailing list, she thought, you were on forever.

Rubbing her hand over the glossy page filled with photos of saddles, Mattie felt a surge of yearning. It wasn't true, she thought, that she didn't need a saddle and bridle. It was true that she had no use for one, but that wasn't the same as not needing one. She reached to turn out the light, her other hand still touching the pictures.

Chapter 19

Spring vacation week came with a rush of warm air. Bits of purple and yellow popped out of dull ground, proud-breasted robins hopped their silly dance, windows were thrust open to refresh furnace-stuffy houses. It was going to be a great week to be home, Mattie thought.

She and Hank stood watching Whisper wheel about the pasture. Chasing butterflies, Hank said, though of course there were no butterflies yet, but Mattie knew what he meant.

Mattie felt calm, like the gentle air around her, more content than she had been since the car crash that had changed everything. Yet some urge she held inside kept her humming to herself, running her hand back and forth across the top fence board.

Whisper was still a bit shaggy, although the winter hair came out at each brushing. She was spirited and lively, a beautiful motion picture. Most days Whisper seemed to feel as good as Mattie felt seeing the mare's improvement.

Hank had stayed quiet beside her. She enjoyed watching him watching the horse he had helped save.

"You know I'm going to ride her someday." Mattie had cocked her head and said it almost teasingly, with a hint of a challenge in it. She could say things to this old man that she didn't dare say to anyone else.

A twitch of smile wiggled at the corner of Hank's mouth, but without taking his eyes off the big horse he answered solemnly, "I know you are."

Mattie felt satisfied. Somehow Hank understood. Maybe she would never get to ride Whisper, but he knew how badly she wanted to, needed to.

"I'm getting muscles," she said and grinned. It was as though she had gotten nowhere for so long, and all at once she was on top of the mountain.

Hank laughed. "Whooee, you are. I swear you've about put dents in the side of that barrel you keep riding, girl."

Mattie rolled her eyes, but then her laughter spilled out, too.

The warm weather stayed through the week like a welcome old friend. Sweatshirt, jeans, and barn boots were all Mattie needed as she spent the glorious days with Whisper.

Now if Whisper rooted around the ground she could actually find new spring grass, but Mattie couldn't allow her in the pasture for very long. "Your stomach has to get used to that rich stuff a little at a time," she told Whisper.

Dr. Klamson came one day to check Whisper's progress. He eased his well-scrubbed hands into the pockets of his blue coverall. "Looks good, still. Better than we could have hoped." He gave Mattie a look she couldn't quite decipher, but she guessed he thought she had done the right thing for Whisper. He patted the horse. "I'm making a report to a research group at the University so they know of at least one more horse this drug seems to have helped. We'd need to get new x-rays to be certain, but my guess is the damage to the navicular bone has been checked."

Maybe they could arrange for x-rays, Mattie wasn't sure. But she wondered, "Is there a chance that the old damage is going away?"

The vet smoothed his wild eyebrows before answering. They seemed the only thing about him he couldn't quite subdue. He shook his head. "No. What's done is done in that case. Permanent. But, keeping the disease in control and making the animal comfortable, that's no small thing, Mattie."

Leaving Whisper in her stall, Mattie walked Dr. Klamson to his truck. As he closed himself inside with a solid thud, he added, "It wouldn't hurt now for Whisper to be ridden lightly. Nothing racy, no jumping, just a small dose of controlled exercise by a thoughtful rider." He waved casually and drove away as though he had said nothing that mattered.

Mattie stood planted there feeling as if her head was going to take off somewhere without the rest of her. She had wanted to ask him about riding but couldn't get it out in the air for him to toss away as any crazy idea deserved. Now he had said yes without being asked.

She wheeled about and flew back to the stall. She hugged Whisper fiercely and felt her own heart pounding against the mare. "If only I could," she murmured.

On Friday morning Mattie finished mucking out and put Whisper back in her stall. Wayne was earnestly whacking a lacrosse ball into the closed barn door, trying to catch the rebound in his racket. Each hit left a half-circle smudge on the door. Mattie had just hollered at him to cut it out—not that she cared all that much, but it was her natural born duty to scold him—when Hank drove up.

"Hi," Mattie greeted him. "Where have you been all week?" She thought he would have been around more while she was on vacation.

Hank hustled toward her. "Been busier than a centipede knitting socks," he exclaimed.

Mattie grinned.

"Come on. See what I got in the truck for you."

Wayne didn't need an invitation. He sprinted ahead of them to get the first look.

Hank called, "Now you hush up, boy," before Wayne could give away the surprise.

Wayne stayed mute, but his face told Mattie this was something special. She turned past the back end of the pickup bed, and there it was. Sitting in the rusty bed like jewels in a cigar box were an English saddle, saddle pad, and bridle.

Hank was short of breath trying to share quickly. "I been hunting around, and I found these finally. They're nowheres near new, but . . . well, I hope they'll be just right for you," he said.

Mattie couldn't say a word. She kept blinking her eyes and rubbing the smooth leather of the saddle and swallowing. In the old days, before the accident, she had circled her choices of tack in catalogues and longed for the day when they would be hers. Hers to put on her own horse; hers to soap and clean and polish; hers to touch every day. She had given up on that, except for the rare times she let herself dream, and now it all lay before her. Good. And beautiful.

Hank couldn't take her silence. "Mattie?" he said hopefully.

With that she threw herself at him, burrowing into his hugeness. "Thank you," she croaked.

When the hugging was over and Hank was laughing his relieved guffaw, Mattie looked again at her perfect gift. A twang of guilt rang through her as she thought Hank couldn't afford this. She turned back to him. His face shone like a polished apple. He looked almost young. Instead of protesting, she quietly said again, "Thank you."

"Well, you're welcome, Mattie. Mighty welcome. Now where is that Whisper?"

Mattie giggled. "In the stall. Stretching out her morning hay as long as she can."

As they started toward her, Wayne snatched at Mattie's arm. His face darkened. "You aren't going to ride Whisper, are you?"

Mattie understood his caring. She had always talked to him of how Whisper couldn't be used. She had never spoken to anyone but Hank about riding Whisper. Now she kind of wished she had shared with Wayne.

She tried to reassure him. "Whisper's so much better.

I'm not going to work her hard, and anyway you've seen how she likes to run."

"It'll hurt her; the vet said!"

Mattie was shaking her head furiously in her need to explain. "I didn't tell the good news. Just this week, he said she can be ridden. That she should be ridden!"

Wayne seemed to be brightening, then another idea hit him. "But you can't ride. You're not supposed to." There was wonder in his voice now.

Mattie held herself very straight. "We'll just see, won't we?" she replied softly. Then urgently, "Go on and get Mom and Dad."

He turned tail and ran to the house, shouting, "Mom... Dad! Mom!"

Hank had taken the halter off and held the bridle ready to be slipped over Whisper's head. She eyed it suspiciously, so he let her look it over a minute. Still she ducked away from it at first. "Been some time since she's had these gadgets on."

"Umhmm," Mattie agreed.

On the second try Whisper allowed Hank to fit the bit into her mouth and slide the band over her ears. He buckled the bridle into place and laid the reins back over Whisper's withers.

Mattie was so intent on the change she was watching, there was no room for talking. Neither did she need to tack Whisper herself this time. Seeing was enough. In the months Whisper had been her horse, she had sometimes imagined her this way. Now Whisper chewed on the bit, and then, seeming satisfied, she turned a look toward Mattie that said "What next?"

Hank carried the rich dark-brown saddle from the truck

and gingerly placed it on Whisper's back. After he had fastened the girth loosely, Whisper craned her neck around to inspect the new item and gave a snort that Mattie hoped was approval.

Mattie gripped the reins, her right hand close under Whisper's chin, and walked the mare into the bright morning light. The air was charged with life, an electricity Mattie hadn't felt for a very long time.

Whisper didn't object to the saddle, so Hank slowly tightened the girth. Mattie led her in a large circle while Hank dragged out the wooden steps he and Wayne had built for her to use with her barrel. They would make a good mounting block. Whisper was prancing more than walking, her head going up and down so much Mattie's arm worked like a pump handle. Mattie could see in that broad face eagerness to match her own.

Mattie climbed the steps that put her belly side to side with Whisper's, reached for the saddle, and stuck her left foot into the stirrup. She inhaled deeply. Just once she thought, Can I do this? Then she pulled with strong arms and swung jerkingly onto her horse. Whisper lurched forward, then backward. Her ears were moving fast, stirring the air. "Ho, girl," Mattie crooned in a low voice. "Everything's fine, Whisper." She felt like hollering but knew that could bring disaster. Strict control was called for here. This horse felt nothing like a barrel.

Mattie saw the family rushing her way. Her mother's hand flew to cover her open mouth, and Dad stopped and stared.

Mattie gathered the reins, her heart floating. At last she was one with her horse. United. With this vital, powerful animal under her, Mattie felt separated from the everydayness of limping over the ground. She could fly!

With her back held straight, legs barely nudging Whisper forward, and heels not quite down, Mattie moved into the open, welcoming pasture.